Wondershrub and Club

Rudy J. Gerber

authorHOUSE®

AuthorHouse™
1663 Liberty Drive, Suite 200
Bloomington, IN 47403
www.authorhouse.com
Phone: 1-800-839-8640

First published by AuthorHouse 12/3/2007

ISBN: 978-1-4343-2842-7 (sc)
ISBN: 978-1-4343-2843-4 (hc)

Printed in the United States of America
Bloomington, Indiana

This book is printed on acid-free paper.

"It is error alone which needs the support of government; truth can stand by itself"
Thomas Jefferson, Notes on Virginia, 1782.

"Political language – and with variations this is true of all political parties, from Conservatives to Anarchists –is designed to make lies sound truthful and murder respectable, and to give an appearance of solidity to pure wind."
George Orwell, "Politics and the English Language," 1946

"Our government is run by an array of authoritarian personalities who are dominating,opposed to equality, desireous of personal power, amoral, intimidating … vengeful, pitiless, exploitive, manipulative, dishonest, cheaters, prejudiced, meanspirited, militant, nationalistic and two-faced."
Nixon lawyer John Dean, Conservatives without Conscience (2006)

Also by Rudolph Gerber

The Insanity Defense

Contemporary Issues in Criminal Justice

Punishment: Views, Explanations, Justifications

The Criminal Law of Arizona

Legalizing Marijuana

The Railroad and the Canyon

Lawyers, Courts and Professionalism: The Agenda for Reform

Dedication

To Trevor and Caroline
Ad multos annos!

Acknowledgements

My wife Kathleen deserves many thanks for enduring my time commitments and ranting on political topics. My friends at Authorhouse have been unfailingly creative with publication and editorial ideas. Morris Dean, my colleagues at the Court of Appeals and at the law firm of Shughart Thomson and Kilroy, and our Phoenix bookclub members – the Noyes, Foreman, and Martone families – gave indirect inspiration. Last, and certainly least but by no means insignificant, George W. Bush and his cronies – so dedicated to proclamations of compassion, decency, human rights, democracy and respect for life -- provided unlimited irony beyond the hopes of any author.

R.J.G.

Contents

1

Inaugural Address of President Wondershrub at the Trick E. Dioxin Presidential Library, San Cement, CA

President Wondershrub lays a wreath at the tomb of the silver-coated tongue of former President Trick E.Dioxin. The <u>Weakly Standard</u> Journalists' Choir intones the theme from "The Rhinestone Cowboy." The President and Vice President Lip Surley stride to the microphone.

President Wondershrub:

My fellow America, I am honored to be with you on this lovely literary day to begin my reign as your forthcoming president. Let me first tell you some of my heroes I will imitate in my administration. One of them you know by name because he held this same office, former President Trick E. Dioxin , so prematurely taken from our mist. I stand here today at this sacred tomb honoring his silver tongue, where I have placed a laurel wreath in memory of his upscale political language. I will follow on that high literary road to achieve the goals his tongue left unsaid because of its prenatal departure from the oral orifice. A tree don't fall far from its acorns. I will be, like him, the "I am not a crook" President.

The other hero of mine, the greatest philosopher of all time in my humbler opinion, is Jesus. It is because of Him that I have chosen compassionate conservatism as the theme of my presidate. I will live up fully to His compassion and respect for all life, without exception, in particular for stem cell life, no matter how microscopic. All human life, from wee little stem cells on up to the choirs of angels, including Seraphim and Cherubim, is sacred, regardless of size, color, race, creed, religion or wing-span.

Let me sharify with you the four main goals of my administration. First, I intend to improve education all the way from our faith-based universities down to the dungeons of the Darth Vader Institute of Ventriloquism, where my Vice President, Lip Surley, serves as the founding dean. If you can't literate, you can't maturate. Silver and gold may pass away but education, like good oil, will never dismay. My administration will distribute bumper stickers saying that no school child will be left behind unsuckled Rarely do we ask ourselves the crucial question, "Why is our children not learning?" Reform must begin with our elementary and high schools and then expand to our grade schools and even to our secondary schools as well. If you teach a child to read, he or her will be able to pass a literary test. If you can't read, it's going to be hard to go to college. I understand that. I experienced it. But I overcame my obstacles and, in fact, just this summer finished reading three illustrated Shakespeares. This nation needs an education system that is next to none, especially regarding the Biblical knowledge of good and evil, the root of the entire Knowledge Tree. Books is important for education, especially books having fantastic action pictures.

To that end, I will be proposing to Congress to turn the Library of Congress into a comic book research center featuring first editions of such classics as Superman and Batman as guides for setting our foreign policy. To start the comics rolling in, I am today making a donation to this library from my own collection of the great comic classic Wonderboy, my personal favorite.

Second, my administration will affirm the dignity of all life , starting with stem cells, the very germs of life. Every embryo is someone's blood relative. Like an unfertilized snowflake, each of these embryos is unique. Just because a stem cell is small or watery or foreign-looking is no reason to deny it the right to life, liberty or the pursuit of happiness. We should not scramble such eggs! We don't do that to eggs. I too was once an egg, though now am unyoked. Perhaps it is the mom in me but stem cells resignate in my breasts. I will propose to Congress to set up a stem cell bank in each Federal Reserve Bank to display stem cells, under glass, in their original frozen condition. These banks will offer special discounted admission for friends and families of folks with impaired stems, like Michael J. Fox, Christopher Reeve, and Stephen

Hawking, as well as any Sturgeon Generals whose stem cell research agrees with me despite contrary scientific data. I will also propose to Congress that we give Republican stem cells the right to vote, so they can exercise a derisive voice in democracy even before they can think. I also hope to create a special exhibit for stem cells in the great religious theme park I envision at our nation's capital. Only one thing could change my mind about preserving stem cells -- if we find they contain oil, because such is a main interest of my Grand Oil Party.

Third, we must reform our climactic values. We need a faith-based climatology where science works for religion, not visa versa. The Book of Guinness, as you Biblical scholars know, gives us dominion over beasts of the air and birds of the fields. Our climate suffers from too many "inconvenient truths" from Mr Oscar Ozone about global warming. These warmings of the earth and the thousands of summertime fires and droughts is less important than warming up our energy engines. We have callings higher than listening to Mr Ozone going about "Teuton his own horn." Remember the story of the Three Little Pigs who solved their environmental problem simply by going to the market, teaching us that going to the market will solve Mr Ozone's inconvenience just as it did for the cute little pigs.

Under my correct climate science, we will be building more pipelines to carry oil to our thirsty market engines. That we are the world's leading producer of fossilized greenhouse gasses requires us to use market forces to keep us in first place. Global warmings and second-hand tobacco smoke are junk sciences, less deserving of being taught in our schools than intelligent designings or Wonderboy comics. We don't need any more so-called scientific facts like this. I will accordingly silence those godless government scientists who discover scientific facts about global warming. You can't make a sow's purse from a Sheik's ear. You can't make the flat earth round by appealing to so-called facts.

The Book of Guinness again offers us an useful amalgam. Behold the lilies of the field: they toil not, neither do they spin, yet each year they bloom like Solomon's morning glories, not only in cold weather but also in hot weather such as ours. We also read in those same scriptures that Adam and Eve felt heat too, even in Paradise, that's why they wore their clothes nudely. Moses himself lived in heat so great the bush before him burnt up. Are you worried about Mr Ozone's global flooding? In the Great Flood Noah had no need to call for govment Arkangels to control the environment; he simply accepted the melting glaciers, put on his boots, got his chain saw, and built and floated his Ark to combat the flood waters. After guiding his Ark to the marketplace, he got himself a job, exactly as the Book of Job teaches! With the use of similar market forces we too, like the Three Little Pigs and Noah and his wife Joan of Arc, can get a job, buy fans and KoolAid, lay pipelines and build our own arks today, even bigger ones, commiserate with the size of any glacier meltings. To that end my Vice President Surley, whispering here at my side, will be directing and starring in "Very Convenient Truthiness," a documentary film memorializing the advantages of global warming for my contributors vacationing at our new Greenland resorts.

Finally, my administration will be offering health savings plans to all Americans, regardless of income levels, in place of govment health coverage. I know your concerns about bigger health costs. I too have a medical body and it costs me too. With my health savings plan, even a minimum wage McDonald's hamburger flipper could save a quarter, perhaps even fifty cents, from each paycheck to put into a health savings account for the common cold or any other financial catastrophe. Health savings plans enable all our people, rich and poor alike, to sleep under the same bridges, eat in the same soup kitchens and pay for their own health problems with personally-owned savings plans identical except as to the amounts. The beauty of this savings plan is that it's open to any savers from a top CEO of a Forbes 500 company right on down to a poor homeless person sleeping under one of those bridges . That's what democracy means: freedom for everyone, regardless of creed or religion, to choose any health plan they can afford.

Under my new health plan each person of every economic level can be a happy health saver. I will replace our inner city mobile medical clinics with mobile information centers where my compassionate health counselors will advise poor folks how to save their hard-earned pennies for such medical disasters. I will also be proposing that Congress authorize pre-paid health care cards, just like pre-paid phone cards, so that even poor people can dial up several minutes of health coverage at a cost of only a few hunnert dollars per second. You can now see why my administration will be known for its compassion for any poor people who camp under the soaring bridges of this nation after welfare families move abroad.

In conclusion, though repetition is unnecessary, by way of closing, let me end by concluding with some final finishing summations. On this happy literary occasion I am proud to announce that I am today donating my personal collection of Pinocchio stories to this Dioxin Library so that the entire world can assess these books whose fantastic pictures about truthiness have made me who I am. I and the entire House of Shrub is honored to presidate over you. I extend an invitation to any qualified American who wants to work in my administration. I certainly do not want Yes-men working around me, but rather people of integrity who will fully agree with my decisions after I make them. I urge you to join with me to refuel our country and embitter it for our predecessors still to come. If you are fed up with the politics of principle, come, join with me. Jackhammer up the pipelines! Pile the pie higher! Vulcanize society! Let's come together to unite!

The <u>Weakly Standard</u> Journalists' Choir concludes the inaugural program by singing "The Man of La Mancha." The President leaves in his Batmobile to attend a Yale University meeting of the committee deciding the Nobel Prize for Literature.

2
Really Unruly of FAUX NEWS Interviews Presidential Advisor Reverend Rover Rasputin

Really Unruly, FAUX NEWS: Let's all welcome today's special guest, Reverend Rover Rasputin! So great to have this opportunity to interview you here on our FAUX network, Reverend, about your creation and marketing of a new explosive line of purgative products modeled, I understand, on potions first developed by your honored namesake, Rasputin, the counselor to the Russian Czar. We've heard daunting accounts of these new products you've produced as part of your work for the Wondershrub administration. We'd like you to give our viewers a fair and balanced account of this controversial new brand and its benefits.

Reverend Rover: Well, thanks so much, Really, and many blessings upon you and your family and our many friends in FAUX viewerland. Yes, it's true that, at the request of our President and Vice President, and in conjunction with our Food and Drug Administration, I have been called to develop this new product line that offers the promise of eliminating both personal and national discomforts. The full generic name for these products is "Rover's Snake Oil Purgative Designer Line," which refers to several purifying products under one label.

Really Unruly: What exactly is this product line, and what is it supposed to do?

Rover: The first is this small canister of this oleaginous liquid diuretic, fortified with herbs and organic compounds from neutered moose once living in the former Alaskan Wildlife Preserve. The diuretic is the very one developed in Imperial Russia by Rasputin himself from a mixture of beets, vodka, and potato peels marinated in decades-old borscht soup flavored with German boar sausage. He used this very formula as an aid for the Czar's own personal difficulties. I have used the same ingredients but increased their potency with a sausage formula I discovered in an old German recipe book, *The Wurst of Nietzsche*. As you know, the great gourmet Friedfood Nietzsche first wrote about these seminal purgative ingredients in his culinary masterpiece *Thus Ate Zarathustra*.

When these combined ingredients are taken as directed by our Sturgeon General in Washington DC, their immediate effect is lubrication of a person's insides, which of course facilitates expelling all traces of liberal elitism. For that reason it's also known by its generic name as a "liberal purgative." Its primary benefit lies in expunging free-wheeling thought patterns from every organ in the body. It starts in the brain and works downward with a trickle-down effect. Taken as directed, it will close all thought pores so they remain uncontaminated by outside air-borne diseases, such as curiosity, questioning, or skepticism, that might disturb the regularity of the body politic.

Really: Astounding! Our country has long needed such a tonic as an alternative to nasty questioning and aggressive finger-pointing. Tell me how you take it.

Rover: "Revered Rover's Snake Oil Liberal Purgative No. 2" is a completely natural product, made from organic oils, herbs, and real Polar Bear fur, and mixed with diluted organic compost from extinct spotted owls, natural in every respect and bio-friendly. A daily recommended 6-liter dose every hour helps to eliminate all blockages to political right-thinking . In the first series of doses it's not unusual for some users to feel disoriented or experience a sense of fullness, even a feeling of being bloated like a whale. The secret lies in resisting these bloated feelings by taking "Rover's Rapid Constiper No. 3."

The best way to do all this is to develop a daily regimen. For example, listen to a fair and balanced news program such as yours while drinking six liters of this purgative No. 4 during every expression of editorial opinion, that is, about 100 liters per half hour. That should get things moving very quickly.

Really Unruly: (*pointing finger*) Hey, Reverend, thanks for the plug; we here at FAUX certainly know exactly where viewers can get this fair and balanced perspective! Tell us more about how your wonderful purgatives work and their expected benefits.

Rover: The original purgative component is not a pill or capsule but a white powder well known to President Wondershrub himself. The President himself has personally endorsed it. All our companion products build upon this white powder base, so you can achieve triumphant purgations with a full dosage of each product. As an example, each of "Reverend Rover's RightMind System" capsules, when taken as a daily serving along with "Reverend Rover's Immediate Solutions Mix," helps to expel faddish values so as to expand space for established traditions. My regimen counteracts heavy diets like yogurts, teas, figs and *the New Yorker*, all well known to cause digestive upset.

Taken in conjunction with "Rover's Politico-Roto" and "Rover's Hourly Bile Blast," available only in "blue state" outlets, these combined purgatives rapidly squelch tendencies to question, complain or even wonder. Instead, these products, taken as directed by right-minded pharmacists in our administration, help restore the absolute docility God intended in order to regulate our citizens' internal compliance mechanisms.

Here are some things a user can expect from taking an hourly mixture of these purgatives: your bile feels relaxed, more expansive, even spacious; your holding patterns are not as lengthy as on major airlines; vomiting and explosive expulsions enable you to resist political elitism; tiny reassuring voices of patriotism are more easily heard and followed; and annoying urges to question, complain, read *the New York Times* or ask "why?" markedly subside. It is true that some patients feel a frequent urge for mind-voiding every five minutes or so. Though this feeling can be distressing at first, when indulged, it allows purged spaces in the brain to adhere tightly to seminal values pre-approved by FDA druggists in our administration. Once these portions are working at full speed, your buttocks begin to march in straight lines and your bile ceases giggling as it babbles over your kidney stones.

In a word, these products, taken as directed by our Dogma Office on Pennsylvania Avenue in Washington DC, remodel your insides from top to bottom, to shape you into a patriotic consumer whose compliant innards qualify you, even as an adult, for an award as a "no child left behind," fully able to digest any pre-packaged doctrine without question, comment, dissent or even thought. In a word, no political indigestion!

Really Unruly: Any side effects, Reverend, and if so, what's to be done about such? We've heard, for example, some rumors that your purgatives may reduce human beings to the docility of sheep.

Rover: The only side effects in animal studies have been diminished curiosity, reduced questioning, increased drowsiness, and a more relaxed libido. Vice President Lip Surley actually took only one dosage and found it quickly eliminated all traces of his diminished libido as well as his hair! Some beginning users have developed unusually stiff necks, a rigid backbone and difficulties moving dogma about. A few have suffered from constipated noses. Some have developed itchy hyenas. But, generally, these complaints have been short-lived and totally consistent with internal compliance. Beginning users usually do best if they start with six to eight liters of our "Roto NumbingAppetizer No. 5" Once these liters are consumed, successful users typically follow political directives without second thoughts or questioning, though occasional leaking sometimes occurs, for which my "Rover's Prophylactic Diapers" serve as a useful beta blocker.

The medical advantage of this line of products, of course, is that the creeping Liberal Elitism Disease, ("LED"), so easily spread from the sickly "blue states," can be diagnosed by my censors in the Centers for Liberal Disease Control, well before these pernicious plagues invade any "red" cells. For the most aggressive regimen I recommend taking six liters of my "Snake Oil Purgative Premium," along with a mouthful of my "RotoMindBlast," for the most lasting emptying. If you feel like you are passing a large jagged object, it's almost certainly your former independent backbone. You won't need a strong backbone with these products. Passing an old backbone is a reliable indication that the consumer has successfully purged an entire Liberal Elite Menu.

Our happiest customers are those who formerly suffered from creeping open-mindedness by reading the Index of Prohibited Doctrines. Some of our most compelling personal testimonials about triumphant expulsions have come from successful converts. In our own country one of my most frequent users is the famous political commentator Ms. Annabelle Nastycolt. She has become an outspoken public model for all my purgatives. For instance, her personal testimonials describe in graphic detail how my "HiOctane Snake Oil Purgation" helped her, and millions like her suffering the heartbreak of lethal   psoriasis, to acquire the acute perception needed to readily identify   political faggots.

You also asked about turning people into docile sheep. If God had not intended our users to be shorn, He would not have made them sheep in the first place. As Ms. Nastycolt's example richly shows, sheep provide us good examples of how to follow the leader while chewing on trash.

Really Unruly: What a wonderful product for helping to return all of us to a simpler, more childlike world, for making us into a tabula rasa where pre-approved doctrines can be inscribed painlessly, even automatically, onto our compliant minds. Is there a way you can test the efficacy of these purgative products?

Rover: Yes, in fact there is an outstanding method.   Doctors certified by our administration to further the medical dogma prescribed by President Wondershrub can perform a specialized procedure known as a nasal colonoscopy, under sedation of course. This is an out-patient procedure done by inserting a FAUX probe into and through the nasal passages up into the brain. This procedure permits druggists loyal to the administration's ear-nose-and-throat   ideology to view both the nasal passages and the brain. They can then cast a loop around any free thinking polyps and can extract them through the mouth by use of a permanent tongue depressor. Certified nasal proctologists then receive these polyp specimens in the National Institute of Dogma Health and submit them for analysis by approved pharmacists working for the Sturgeon General in the Centers for Liberal Disease Control. All this, of course, is performed under anesthesia.

One beneficial effect of these medical procedures is to suppress a patient's tendencies for opening the mouth or other head orifices to contaminating ideas. We begin with the mouth because that's the prime suspect in spreading sickly ideas. As you should know, opening the mouth for speaking one's mind allows invasive liberal germs to spread into the nasal passages, travel to the brain and threaten compliant mental functioning. Would you like me to schedule a nasal colonoscopy for you, Really, or perhaps order you a supply of extra-large tongue depressors? Or a refill of anesthesia?

Really: No, thanks, Reverend. I have had my liberal polyps removed years ago. And no tongue depressors fit my tongue, and I've plenty anesthesia left. Thanks so much for appearing on our show today with information about these new medical devices for controlling the body's openings to contaminating ideas.

Rover: Operators are standing by to take your orders at the end of this program. Order a beginning supply for your friends and family members, to keep them mentally and emotionally compliant for four years at a time, with another four year renewal at only modest charge. Callers who act now will receive their choice of an eight - year supply of tranquilizers personally blessed and autographed by Reverend Rasputin myself or an eight-year bonus of the Best of Zarathustra's Mind-Numbing Wurst. Amen, and eternal rest to all the faithful!

3
Declaration of War Against Iraq

An Address to the American people delivered jointly by President Wondershrub and Field Marshall Rumpelstilskin at Messiah University's Tomb of The Four Unknowing Soldiers of the Apocalypse.

The President emerges from the university's steroid - secure locker room to stand on the dais between the Field Marshall and Vice President, who are embalmed in a cluster of American and NASCAR flags. Presidential Advisor Reverend Rover Rasputin leads the Rover Liturgical Dancers in a spirited <u>pas de deux</u> on the podium. The Messiah Chorale, directed by Secretary Heartfelt, hums "Onward Christian Soldiers" as the President approaches the cross-shaped microphone.

President Wondershrub:
My Fellow Americorns, as well as Christians everywhere, I am happy to be invited here on "Church Lady Day" at this great uniracial institution, on this lovely spring day that brings all major sexes together, to dedicate this statue in her honor and to inaugurate our evangelical crusade against the pagan country of Iraq.

Before getting into that important news, I have the happy task of recognizing some friendly faces here in the audience. Secretary of State Brunette Brunhilde is here. Inspector General Alonzo Gonzo is also here, as are Vice President Lip Surley whispering at my side, as usual. Betsy Ross is again doing her talents at the organ with the national flagsong. The Charwoman of the Joint Chefs of Staff stands here on the podium again offering large-sized testosterone hors d'oeuvres, so tasty that one is never enough. Our loyal NASCAR and NRA officials have also joined us, along with my Supreme Court friends, Justices Scorpio and Scorpiolini, holding those lovely red-white-and-blue candles. And this lovely Chorale honors us all by singing the ever-

13

new biblical Song of Songs with lyrics by Reverend Rasputin himself! A volley of High Fives to all of you!

I am especially happy to announce to you today that the House of Shrub is donating funds to this university to establish 666 annual Turd Blossom Fellowships in honor of my friend and advisor, Reverend Rover himself. By the way, the Reverend is today offering special discounts on his entire line of Liberal Oils of Purgation ("LOPS"). You can inspect his products afterwards at the table by the restrooms. I also wish to acknowledge his sacred Liturgical Dancers in their patriotic red tutus.

This university is a special place for me. It is here at this university where our carefully selected Turd Fellows will conduct cutting-edge research on how universities such as this can use scriptural language for political goals, thereby ending any conflict between science and religion. May God continue to bless these carefully chosen Turd Fellows!

Now let's talk war. I have previously announced to you, the American peoples, my administration's policy of preemptive strikes against any outside threat to our country. Preemptive means we get the first turn in attacking even without declaring war, indeed even without provocation. If this strikes some of you as rash, you need to learn to place your trust in the Unilateral . Unilateral means making decisions quicker and cheaper than talking in Towers of Babel like Congress or the United Nations. Our enemies never stop thinking about new ways to harm our country, and neither do we.

We know there are WMD in Iraq. The sketches of our intelligence agencies confirm that fact. These sketches show these weapons sitting secretly in the large white trailers in downtown Baghdad. We know from our purified intelligence that Al Qaeda weapons hide there as well, quite likely in Osama's bidet. (*flumbles his 3x5 index cards, sits on Vice President Surley's lap and adjusts microphone*)

You may wonder what it means to "purify" our intelligence. While I cannot tell you anything at all about that, because all government actions remain top secret, I can tell you that this technical term requires separating out those facts useful for our goals from those that are not. To purify our intelligence means to cherry-pick those spy pieces we want to use based on what we want to do. All other leakings is anti-American because leaking govment information to the public in a democracy upsets our citizens' sense of tranquility.

Even if these trailers turn out to be empty again, even every time we sketch them, we know they can quickly fill up with WMD in future sketches, as Secretary Nostradamus and his elite intelligence agencies prove simply by re-doing their drawings There's an old Texas expression among spy agencies, "If at first you don't succeed, sketch, sketch again."

So, with this background, and for these compelling reasons, I decided today, once and for all, while weight-lifting this morning with the Field Marshall, to declare a holy crusade against Iraq. To make peace we must first make war. I have more than one reason for doing so. War is needed not only to revenge 9/11 but also to seize the WMD our sketches show are hiding in those empty white trailers, hiding exactly like Osama. Another reason is what Mr Sodom and Ms Gomorrah tried to do to my daddy. Sodom is my daddy's unfinished Iraq business. I can do better than my daddy by completing the war he started and the Sodomites he left uncaught. This war against the Iraqi heathens may even permit us to retake the Garden of Eden from the pagans who have camped out there as squatters ever since Adam and Eve left Cain and Abel behind to marry and propagate our race.

We will be supported in this holy crusade by a vast cotillion of wheeling nations determined to spread democracy to the whole world by no more force than necessary. This war will prove that, unlike a prior occupier of this office, no wimp will ever again sit in the oval chair in the oral office. I will achieve in this war what my daddy failed to do: separate Sodom from his wife Gomorrah, pursuant to the Book of Guinness, and restore order to Iraq and its sacred oil to us.

Field Marshall Rumpelstilskin now has a few words about how this war will deliver shock and awe to Iraq's Palace Sodomites and quick happiness for our own nation. I'll turn over the mike to you, Mr. Marshall Field.

Field Marshall Rumpelstilskin: Thank you, Mr. President. I too am delighted to be with you and your friends today, including the assembled honor guard of the Cockfighters of America, as well as the wonderful college chorale on this sunny spring day who are singing in honor of this school's "Church Lady Day." In this war we have just

15

declared, our country will be supported by what our president has just called a "cotillion of the willing" of many other freedom-loving nations.

British soldiers in the great traditions of the Pirates of Penzance and HMS Pinafore will join with us, led by Britain's Prime Minister, Sir Tophat Poodle. Sir Tophat has been solidly behind us in this decision to go to war right from the very first alteration of memos between our two countries, well before any superfluous United Nations debate. He will join with this administration as a co-partner in this crusade along with other willing nations who, with only modest financing from our government, will impose democracy on every piece of land our soldiers touch, using only the minimum force necessary.

Up-to-date intelligence from Secretary Nostradamus and from Vice President Surley's private libido confirms that our troops will be greeted in Baghdad by throngs of cheering civilians waving garlands and roses. Our advance gardeners from the 6th Gardening Battalion have already slipped into Iraq and, even as we speak, are now diligently enriching the soil in all major Iraqi cities for flower gardens, figs and olives. At this hour, as I speak to you, these peace-loving gardeners are arranging red-white-and- blue daisies for brightly-colored garlands to place around our soldiers' necks as they enter Baghdad in a triumph of what my PR department calls "shock and awe."

Though the legal aspects of war are less important, of course, for impressing other nations than battlefield triumphs , they deserve some mention so we don't get bogged down with bad PR later. This administration will fully comply with the Geneva Convention on the treatment of prisoners, including humane treatment, easy access to lawyers and courts, even for Sodom and Gomorrah. These prisoners will enjoy unlimited virtual contacts with visiting Red Cross mediums. My friend Justice Scorpio, who is singing his touching opera arias here today, assures me our nation's courts will find no legal problem with any POW torture, provided it is no more painful than necessary.

Rest assured that we will operate only humane prisons; the word "gulag" will never be spoken by anyone in this administration. I consider this obligation to reflect your well known compassion, Mr President, and that of your entire administration, regarding respect for all human life beginning even with our brave stem cells, none of whom, by the way, will be forced to fight on the front lines in Iraq against their consciences. Indeed, we expect the war to end well before they can use their GOP voting cards.

Mr President, I know you wish to add a few concluding words.

President Wondershrub: Thank you, Master Marshy Field . Compassionate treatment of all life, including stem cells, indeed remains a defining mark of this administration even in wartime. Accordingly, I am today signing an executive order giving supervision over any prisoners of war and enemy combatants to Inspector General Alonzo Gonzo. He will show the world a compelling example of how this administration values all life forms, from the lowest enemy combatant like Sodom up to the highest single stem cell, just as I promised in my inaugural address at the tomb of the silver tongue of President Dioxin. Compassionate   treatment of prisoners, as Winston Churchill once stated, stands as the surest mark of a civilized society, proving once again that a man and a pig can coexist, just like Tyre and Sidon.

We intend, of course, that this administration remain a beacon of human rights and compassion around the world, even to pigs, for they too have a right to life and libertine happiness. Inspector General Gonzo, too, shares these porcine values; he too believes that cruel, inhumane and degrading treatment of foreign prisoners during wartime always remains improper on our American soil and certainly contrary to the universal compassion defining my administration.   Foreigners, of course, deserve the utmost respect. Foreigners are very important to us – our imports increasingly come from them.

Because it is legally improper to torture foreign prisoners on our own soil, Inspector Gonzo will devise a plan with the CIA to outsource prisoners needing torture to foreign lands via frequent flier flights, all prepaid and at no charge to these passengers. I can assure you that our sacred American soil will never be besotted by any such torture. He will also head a cabinet-level position to coordinate any present and future torture scandals involving our prison personnel as well as to issue any necessary White House denials.   While some of these porcine prisoners may seem to be human beings of only slightly less value than stem cells, we must never forget, as Jesus reminds us in the Song of Solomon, that they are also foreign enemies who come to bring us not peace but a sword. To those Axles of Evil who see it differently, I need say only two words: Bring 'em on! Nobody messes with the House of Shrub!

I know there are criticizers out there who will complain about going to war on the Sabbath or even on this beautiful "Church Lady Day." I know that. I also know that this will be a crusade perhaps difficult for a C student . Some criticizers even say it may also turn out to be an expensive war. But I can assure all our American peoples of all colored creeds that high intelligence has nothing to do with commanding in chief. As to costs, we will not fund this war by raising taxes of our hard-working laborers; in fact, we will cut taxes from our upper income earners and from the patriotic oil companies whose pumpings return the Grand Oil Party only a meager millions in profits each minute.

These tax savings will trickle down from top to bottom , so that even the poorest among us can share in this war's compassionate costs. Any needed funds will also come from the monies saved from individual health savings plans of our poorest terminally-ill Americans of all economic and health levels. If these savings turn out to be insufficient, only then will I ask Congress to sell off Newfoundland or Nova Scotia or, as a last resort, to impose a modest tourist tax on our immigrant workers fanning our donors sunbathing on our popular Greenland beaches. Rest assured that Texas will never be sold.

Our country's policy interests lie in the effort to find those who would harm us and get them out of harm's way. The State of our Union stands united in its very unity. The Great Carpenter Jesus Himself wrote in his Book of Job that a nation divided unto itself should not cast the first stone, just as He also reminds Mr Oscar Ozone, to this very day, of the true picture of his supposed global warming: many are cold but few are frozen.

Therefore, in finishing, let me end by closing with a final conclusion as the last word in this fitting finale. Let me share with you a personal admission. While waging war is a hard decision -- I know that, I am concernful of that -- this important decision today allows me personally, finally, to serve my country in uniform as I have longed to do from my college days bravely serving on weekend drills in the National Guard. When I was a little boy I sent in cereal boxtops for a Sky King glow-in-the-dark ring with a secret compartment plus a decoder for secret intelligence information. I was the first kid on my block with this ring. I proudly carried it with me in all National Guard combat drills until I quit. I proudly wear that ring on my wedding finger to this day. Vice President Surley has one on his member too, though I got mine first. This war offers me what I have always dreamed to do but was unable because other priorities like sports and girls and white powder interfered with my military service: it gives me my first chance to wear in combat my Sky King Ring's Decoder and Secret Compartment, a compartment whose capacity for secrets is exceeded only by that of the Vice President's secret compartments.

I am honored this day to announce to the Americorn People my decision to donate my duplicate Roy Rogers, Gene Autry and Tom Mix comics to this university to inaugurate its new glass-enclosed Wondershrub Memorial Cowboy Comics Collection. I hope future generations of viewers of these fantastic pictures will spread my "don't mess with me" message to others and, in the process, acquire a lasting literary love such as me.

We can take a few questions from the press.

Q Little Sir Echo, FAUX NEWS: Mr Beloved President, how many hours or days or perhaps weeks at the most do you expect this war will last? Will our troops, Your Honor, be home and gathered around the hearth by Christmas? Can our studios help your cause, Your Worship, by spreading fear or perhaps handing out yellow ribbons to be put on old oak trees?

A: President Wondershrub: What would Roy Rogers or Gene Autry or Tom Mix do? That is the guiding policy question. We know this holy crusade against the Sodomites will be very short, hardly even deserving the name of a "war." That's why we have named this the "Hunnert Days Operation." Mr Field Marshall Rumpelstilskin expects our brave fighting men and women to be home in a matter of only a few months at most. As for the yellow ribbons, bring em on! Here are some to hang in your TV studios (*hands out yellow ribbons*).

Q Bear Blitzkreig, CANNED NEWS: Mr Field Marshall, a question for you, sir: John Dean, your fellow conservative and former lawyer for President Dioxon, has written a new book entitled

Conservatives without Conscience, which says, and I quote, that this administration is "run by an array of authoritarian personalities who are dominating, opposed to equality, desireous of personal power, amoral, intimidating … vengeful, pitiless, exploitive, manipulative, dishonest, cheaters, prejudiced, mean spirited, militant, nationalistic and two-faced." Do you think this is an accurate description of your administration?

A: Field Marshall Rumpelstilskin: My Goodness, you'd certainly have to disagree with the part about being two-faced. We can put on as many faces as are necessary.

4

Declaration of Victory in Iraq

The President parachutes from an Apache helicopter, its guns blazing, directly onto the old quadrangle adjoining the ROTC building at Yale University. He strides to a battery of microphones and TV cameras under a large banner proclaiming "Lilies Gilded!" He wears his Wonderboy cape, chrome sunglasses, cowboy boots and a Texas Ranger hat. His cape bears a red-white-and-blue neon sign flashing "In God We Trust." He stands next to Vice President Lip Surley, their ring fingers' secret compartments touching. The Pentagon Cheerleading Team, led by Reverend Rasputin, somersaults over the lilies on the quadrangle green. The Charwoman of the Joint Chefs serves the podium guests testosterone cocktails and platters of hors d'oeuvres spiked with trenbolene for bovine muscle-building.

The president of Yale places an academic hood on the President's shoulders and confers on him a Doctorate in Literature (D. Litt.), <u>honoris causa,</u> for his unique contributions to the English language. Mr Justice Scorpio intones middle C on his harmonica and leads the Supreme Court choir in singing the "Wondershrub Victory News" to the tune of the Notre Dame Victory March:

Cheer, Cheer, for our Wondershrub
Open the comics cheering his name
Send the cannon balls on high
Rain down Apaches from the sky
What though insurgents be great or small
Our Commander in Chief wins o'er them all,
While Sodom and Gomorrah are reeling
From the pangs of victory.

President Wondershrub:

My fellow Americorns, and my friends here at Yale, I thank you for the high literary honor of this D. Litt degree you have conferred on me today. It recalls the honor given to the silver tongue of former President Dioxin that continues to inspire my literary interests as a defining watermark of my administration. This honor is also special for me because it is one you did not see fit to confer on my daddy, though his grades in English and Speech here were better than mine.

I have chosen to parachute peacely from my Air Force Apache helicopter right here on this university triangle to announce the exciting news that, just as promised, and only a few weeks after it started, all offensive operations in Iraq have ended. I stopped them because we won. The Biblical promise of the hunnertfold has come true! Recall the lilies of the field and how they toil no longer, and yet not even Solomon could do better than I in glorifying their toiling. I am honored to tell you that all the lilies in the Iraqi garland gardens have now been fully gilded! Our mission in Iraq is accomplished! Our victory proves that even a C student can win a Middle East war, and even gild their lovely lilies, which is more than my daddy did .

In the very heart of Iraq, we have more exciting news. I am pleased to report to you that, as of today, the Iraqi death toll is well under 80,000 civilians, most of them idle pagans lounging in gutters amid rubble. None of our precious American stem cells have been lost; in fact, not a one has had to leave his or her fortified Petri dishes. Another piece of exciting news that we have saved for this election year is that we have found Sodom himself hiding in his hidey-hole . Yes, he is now capsulated! That, too, is more than my daddy did.

There is even more exciting news . Today, sailors of the 7th fleet landing at the junction of the Tigres and Euphrates Rivers from the nuclear submarine USS Caring, came ashore , toppled the unsavory Pillar of Salt in Baghdad, and took peaceful possession of the original Garden of Eden. All this was done without firing a shot at the Guardian Angels standing guard there.

Let me tell you some more good news (*drops his index cards, sits on the Vice President's lap and adjusts microphone*). A millennium of peace and democracy awaits the joyous Iraqi survivors. Our green gardeners who sneaked into Iraq well before the arrival of our invading troops have been planting even more red roses and daisies for placing around our soldiers' necks as well as on the white tablecloths at the fine dinings in Iraq's many five-star restaurants. Thanks to our awesome invasion, Iraq is fast becoming a country well known for these cheerful garlands and for its Condé Nast tourist amenities like gilded lilies in every five-star hotel room!

I have just received even more wonderful news on my Sky King message decoder. Just today, in the Garden of Eden, troops of the First Faith-Based Battalion occupied the large intersection of Mohammed Blessings Drive and Allah Forever Circle. On that spot they found what Intelligence Secretary Nostradamus has just confirmed is the original Tree of Knowledge of Good and Evil. This lovely Tree is very old, of course, but still has some of its fig leaves. Nearby, on a well worn path leading to the fallen Pillar of Salt, our intelligence services confirm finding the original Apple of this Eden Garden .

Of course, this Apple is somewhat wrinkly as you would expect for an apple of its age, given the many decades since its illegal plucking from the Knowledge Tree. Secretary Johnny Appleseed of our Office of Homeland Orchards tells me that our intelligence agents are returning this Apple to our nation's capital, baked in an airtight diplomatic pie, for careful analysis by Secretary Nostradamus and his forensic fruit experts. Thereafter it will be gilded and put on display for a few days on the windowsill adjacent to my oval office. I will then entrust it to Vice President Surley for safekeeping because of his personal libido for apples as well as his interest in the Tree of Knowledge memoralizing the importance of knowing Good from Evil, Evil from Good, and if not both, then neither. Knowing about morals is a great interest to both of us, including the Vice President. He and I often get drunk on moral Merlot.

You may well ask how we know that this wrinkled Apple constitutes the original Apple plucked from the Tree of Knowledge of Good and Evil. The answer is that handwriting experts in the FBI, CIA, NSA, and Homeland Orchard Office, after repeated microscopic inspections using Apple computers, have found the initials "A" and a smaller "E" carved in Latin right onto its skin In fact, the A and E has a cute heart right between them. Though these initials have somewhat paled with age, the bite marks appear to be those of protruding female teeth.

Nearby the spot of the Apple's discovery our intelligence agents have also found a set of female dentures containing tiny Apple bits that Eve's toothpicks apparently overlooked.

There is even more good news. One of our advance green grocers mulching in the Iraqi victory gardens has found a worn Rib near the same site. It would not be prudent for me at this early stage of our intelligence to speculate that this is the very Rib taken from the side of Adam and used to fashion Eve, the mother of Cain and Abel who, as you know, generated our entire Bible Belt. While any definite conclusion about the Rib would be premature at this point, Secretary Nostradamus does tell me that this is a compelling possibility because of the Rib's male genitalia.

As commander in chief over you and the entire world, I be especially proud of our intelligence personnel and also of you too, Mr. and Mrs. American Front Porch, for your unquestioning trust in the inspiring Bible stories I generously share with you. Of course much still remains to be done in Iraq. Though Adam's Apple has been found, as well, perhaps, as his very own Rib , the WMD have not yet appeared. We are confident they soon will be. We suspect they were there in the Eden Garden in the white mobile trailers placed there by the Avenging Angel who drove Adam and Eve out, just as I have taken out Sodom from his hidey-hole, as my daddy failed to do.

True, these suspicious trailers continue to be empty. That emptiness is exactly what makes them so suspicious: if they are empty, they can then be easily filled up. Our intelligence officials tell us that Sodom's palace guard, the feared and trusted Elite Sodomites, may have moved the WMD from the trailers to a different location on foreign soil, perhaps somewhere in Old Europe, as European senior citizens like to call their ancient country. Our intelligence sketches again show us the voids where they lie hidden, like baby Moses, among the water lilies of the field. We are checking this possibility out with Sir Tophat Poodle and our allied co-partners, whom Vice President Surley is even now wiretapping for this information.

My doctrine of "Trust Me" has paid capital dividends that I intend to spend. Thanks to our Iraq victory gardens and the gilding of its lilies, as well as these awesome Biblical discoveries, we can now breathe a breath of fresh error. We are already seeing the fruits of this Hunnert

Days War. The greatest benefit is right here close to home: the border relations between Mexico and Canada and other Gulf Coast nations are now the best they have ever been, with the sole exception of Venezuela, where our intelligence predicts that President Beelzebub will belch on for only a short time. But aside from that, these friendly neighbors of ours in Central and South America assure me they have no problems at all with my Patriot Act.

We will take a few questions.

Q Little Sir Echo, FAUX TV: O Beloved President, have there been any American deaths? Have you, Your Majesty, had to sign any sad condolence letters to families?

A President Wondershrub: I'm happy you asked that, Sir Echo. Of course, and sadly, there have been a few deaths, but happily much fewer than next to none. We do not know the exact number of American deaths because none of our soldiers' arriving caskets can be counted or photographed so there's really nothing deadly certain to worry about. Our own morbidities are nowhere near as numerous as the joyous Iraqi civilians have suffered, which are well under 80,000, and rising at a slower rate now that the hunnert days is up.

Anyone concerned about these thousands of unfortunate civilian deaths should know that during all the hunnert days of this operation, for a period of 24/7, I was in continuous contact with the several hunnert Iraqi morgues and its thousands of new emergency rooms and cemeteries via an open email connection in case anyone brought to any of these places wished to email me directly or even to contact me personally at my home in Texas via the Pony Express. It is, of course, not my fault that no one took advantage of my compassionate willingness to comfort these folks in their hour of need.

Compassion is indeed the high watermark of my administration. These losses of life seem a fair price for the joyous liberation we have brought to Iraq. Thankfully, none of our stem cells have been lost at all; all our eggs remain safe in their heavily fortified egg dishes. Their yoke remains easy and their burden light. They toil not, neither do they spin. Not even Solomon was yoked like unto them!

As to the condolences, our administration's compassion appears in the many hundreds of sympathy cards personally signed by Field Marshall Rumpelstilskin and me using our new automatic signature machines. The Field Marshall's staff has also sent cute bouquets of four leaf clovers to the families of our 3500 deceased soldiers. Recall the lilies of the field: they toil not, neither do they spin, but not even Solomon in all his glory was buried with garlands of four-leaf clovers such as our buried soldiers. Any more tough questions?

Q Mr Quiz Kid, Elite TV: Some have said that extremism is strengthened by your actions in Iraq, as though our military presence in that country increases the rage of insurgents.

A President Wondershrub: What would the Lone Ranger do? What would his sidekick Tonto do? I remind you and them too that we were not in Iraq on Sept 11, 2001, when Al Qaeda attacked us after invading Iraq. Your comment itself is extreme.

Q Mr Quiz Kid: But, Mr President, Al Qaida was based elsewhere. We were attacked on 9/11 not by Al Qaeda but by the Talliban.

A President Wondershrub: Those countries are both in the Middle East. Our intelligence shows that they are for all practical purposes interchangeable, like Adam and Eve, two peas hiding in the same terrorist pod .

Q. Little Sir Echo, FAUX TV: Why in your wisdom, My Lord, do you think our dedicated fighting men and women have not yet found Bin Laden ?

A President Wondershrub: Because he's hiding in his own hidey-hole, probably in some terrorist cell pod in some friendly country like Belgium. The Vice President and I are determined and indeed confident that we will find him, capsulate him, and give him the ultimate punishment he deserves for what he and Shakespeare's Caliban have done to us in Iraq.

Q Reverend Sarducci, Word Eternal News: You say you are a compassionate conservative. Who would Jesus bomb?

A President Wondershrub: We'll never know because He did his bombing miraculously, without having to use any airplanes.

Q Miss Highbrow, Academic TV: You invaded Iraq because of the assumed WMD there. Now we know that Iran and North Korea both have real WMD, including real nuclear bombs that are pointed our way. Does not your Iraq logic about WMD require invading those two countries or at least bombing them? Or perhaps working with the same United Nations you disavowed regarding Iraq ?

A President Wondershrub: War is not logic. The WMD are like quantum theory – they appear and disappear like waves and participles. My decision to go to war is not one of logic but experience. I be the Decider. These nuclear countries do not sit in the same league as countries with weapons of mass destruction like we know Iraq has hidden in those white trailers. The sketches our intelligence agencies draw on our official easels clearly show these weapons are there. As for the United Nations, we always prefer diplomacy to unilateral action, just as we did in starting the Hunnert Days War. Why, the Lone Ranger himself never hurt anyone unnecessarily and certainly never ignored any United Nations resolutions against Tonto.

As to allied help, intimate relationships are another hallmark of this administration. You may recall, for example, that when I was last in Germany meeting Chancellor Merkel, I gave her a surprise intimate neck massage to loosen her shoulder and neck muscles. I learned how to do that with my fraternity buddies at Yale. I plan to give body massages to all our friendly foreign leaders.

Q Bear Blitzkreig, *CANNED News*: Some critics say that you keep up the pretense of war so you can acquire wartime powers beyond those of peacetime, so, for example, you can wiretap without court order or imprison without charges or trials, and torture whomever you wish.

A President Wondershrub: You don't begin to know your own Constitution. When our Founding Fathers and Mothers sat down in the Justice Department at Runnymeade with King John to write our Constitution, they wrote the Fourth Commandment to forbid wiretaps without court order inside a man's castle. No castles are involved in this war except the one where Osama is hiding. Under the Magnum Carta Sec. 45, wiretaps are limited to American citizens and foreign leaders like Sir Tophat Poodle, for which a court order is required, which we will get just as soon as he requests it.

Let's now move on to happier topics. Mr Field Marshall Rumpelstilskin has taken a lot of heat about his conduct of this war. I know that The Pentagon has prepared a newsworthy press statement that is being released today on his voluntary retirement as he becomes an "emeritus" field marshall . This press statement also reflects the views of my administration about keeping him in office, just as I promised before I removed him. Let's offer him our congratulations as we listen to his press release.

White House Press Secretary Whiteout strides to the podium in the Disco Room of the Department of Euphemisms. He chants in Gregorian Plainsong: I will now read the press release issued today by the Office of Field Marshall Rumpelstilskin Emeritus, after which the Field Marshall will take a few questions:

A Triumph for Field Marshall Rumpelstilskin Emeritus

As he prepares to return to private life, a little more than three short years after the Iraq invasion – a decision that prompted much public criticism of Field Marshall Rumpelstilskin – the Field Marshall with modest pride admits that he is now riding a rising tide of respect and admiration among his colleagues in the nation's capital as well as the world's capitals, as well as with the average GI in Iraq trenches.   As Secretary of State Brunhilde put it recently, "You have to admire this man, seemingly so much more heroic than life itself , for sticking to his decisions in the face of endless criticism from many experienced generals and combat veterans lacking a reading knowledge of the most basic elements of modern warfare. We have no better friend among field marshals."

Secretary Brunhilde's comments represent a wide variety of typical compliments coming to the Field Marshall from around the globe. In Iraq itself, Prime Minister Mohammed Al-Mohammed, who presides over a diverse coalition of religious groups now cheerfully united in rebuilding that country, says he finds the Field Marshall's expertise indispensable for restoring the Iraqi pipelines to full production, as they now are.

Iraq, he proudly reports, is generating a steady flow of oil revenue without any intervention or assistance from the United States except from the Field Marshall's help in setting up the pipeline control centre at the White House. The Arab insurgents have folded up their tents and simply drifted away.   The Prime Minister adds that these accomplishments make it possible for Iraq to flourish as a united, terror-free country now that all insurgents have drifted away. The Iraq economy will rise to the top rung this year in the Middle East. These have been the Field

Marshall's goals from the very first. Gas prices in the United States are already down to a mere 18 cents per gallon.

The Field Marshall's office adds that these Iraqi financial and military accomplishments will make it possible for the United States to inaugurate further tax reductions and to balance its books, even to put the this country in black ink again by the end of the fiscal year. Eliminating the American national debt, once thought nearly impossible because of this administration's tax cuts, seems a foregone conclusion by year's end, thanks to the Field Marshall's cost-saving measures in Iraq within the past 12 months. Indeed, the Field Marshall shares the views of President Wondershrub and Vice President Surley that our entire tax system can be abolished before the end of the year.

The highly disciplined Iraqi army, once nearly destroyed by Saddam's tyrannical rule, appears as the biggest success story for the Field Marshall, This army represents a deserved confirmation of his carefully wrought plan for victory. Immediately after the allied invasion, Iraqi soldiers happily returned to their posts, a strategic move approved by the Field Marshall himself, who several times assured the Iraqis of the American commitment to quickly ending torture there and restoring democracy . The strength of the US- backed Iraqi troops has deterred, seemingly forever, the now impotent Sharks and Jets insurgencies, which are now in their last throes. Bin Laden's reputed recent capture, plus the assassination of his top lieutenant Mohammad Ali, now appear as additional badges of honor on the Field Marshall's spiked helmet.

Within but a few weeks of the invasion, coalition forces raced quickly to capture Baghdad in the successful "shock and awe" campaign designed by the Field Marshall himself . This much celebrated "shock and awe" campaign has indeed been especially awesome for Iraqi civilians. In the early campaign Lot's Pillar of Salt toppled to the ground to the cheers of the city residents. American and coalition troops were welcomed by cheering housewives and schoolchildren who greeted them with Iraqi flags, figs, olives, Islamic prayer books and garlands of freshly gilded lilies.

The Field Marshall also played a major role in directing his troops to the successful re-taking of the Garden of Eden and finding the famous Adam and Eve Apple described in the Christian scriptures. The Field

Marshall says he even personally hopes the Garden can be opened as a sort of Iraqi Everglades once it is transported to the US,   and made accessible to both national and international tourists for only a modest fee that should be waived, he recommends, for our coalition's maimed war veterans.

The Field Marshall says that the sweetest victory for him personally is the reversal of the hostility directed at him by the capitals of "Old Europe" that once ridiculed him. His standing has soared throughout both parts of Europe, old and new, especially in steroid sauna clubs and weightlifting circles . Today he is much sought-after as a humorous after-dinner speaker.   Rumors in intellectual circles say that he is a top candidate for next year's Nobel Peace Prize.   The President himself has nominated him for a seat on the Desmond Tutu Peace and Reconciliation Commission.   One of his proudest honors is that Vice President Lip Surley has just nominated him as this year's recipient of the National "Cockfighter of the Year Award."

Asked to explain his ability to turn vision into reality, the Field Marshall, with typical modesty, says simply "Stuff Happens." He also proudly says that he has no need for using steroids except when he plays war games.

We appreciate your attention to this Press Release on behalf of the Field Marshall. We can take a few questions.

Little Sir Echo, FAUX NEWS: What a press release and what a crime story! What an insight into our Iraq successes! We'll make this press release our headline news on FAUX NEWS ALERT today!

Q: Curious George, CANNED NEWS NOW: Mr Field Marshall Emeritus, one quick question if you please: could you tell us, Sir, how you became a Republican?

A: Field Marshall: My goodness gracious, why, sure, my daddy, my granddad, and my great granddad were all Republicans, so that made it easier.

Q: Curious George: But sir, suppose that your daddy, your granddad, and your great granddad were all horse thieves – what would you then be?

A: Field Marshall: Why,   then,   it'd be even easier to be a Republican.

5

Decision of the Supreme Court of the United States in the case of Abu Gharib and Guantanamo Inmates v. President Wondershrub and Field Marshall Rumpelstilskin, Emeritus.

The Supreme Court's decision is read orally by its author, Associate Justice Antediluvian Scorpio, standing in the robing room of his Supreme Court Star Chambers:

SCORPIO, JUSTICE

The origin of this case lies in complaints against the Wondershrub Administration by ungrateful prisoners of war and dissatisfied enemy combatants, well after the declared end of the brief Iraqi campaign, of being tortured by German Shepherd dogs, clubs and whips, forced to play king of the hill naked, beaten by our peaceloving guards, soiling the red-white-and- blue striped uniforms generously given them, and denied sleep, rest, food, recreation and access to attorneys and courts. These ungrateful prisoners – all foreigners, foreign indeed to our generous American hospitality – seek to invoke American law for protection against the compassionate captors they imagine are somehow torturing them.

No place for foreigners exists under our law. American law applies to Americans, who alone may invoke it. The great rights enshrined in our Constitution are universal to all human beings everywhere who are Americans. Put in technical legal terms, human rights extend up to but not beyond the borders of the sovereign country granting those rights. That is precisely what sovereignty means to those, like me, who serve it faithfully. We recognize no human rights in these foreign combatants because, unlike stem cells, while these foreigners are arguably human, their origins lie beyond our borders, making them guests in our country. As the Romans put it so well about guests, *Hospis venit, Christus venit, crucifige eum!*

These Petitioners' claim under the "cruel and unusual" punishment prohibition of the Eighth Amendment requires that this Court explore the original meanings of the words "cruel and unusual" at the time of that amendment's adoption to determine if their torture today is permitted . When that amendment was adopted in 1791, our Founding Fathers and Mothers (I am by no means sexist) copied it verbatim from the 1689 Bill of Rights of Great Britain, the same country whose troops, thanks to Sir Tophat Poodle, bravely fight alongside ours in Iraq—even after the declared end of that war -- under the virtual inspiration of Field Marshall Rumpelstilskin Emeritus, a friend of mine, whom I have, incidentally, just nominated for this year's Nobel Peace prize. Our country has long enjoyed a suckling relationship with our Mother Country. When we imbibed its constitutional values we also internalized the exact meanings those constitutional words enjoyed at the time of their adoption. "Cruel and unusual" meant to the English in 1689 that persons disloyal to the Crown like the traitor Titus Oats could be whipped and have his skin torn out before his eyes every day for the rest of his life, and that such punishment was <u>customary at the time!</u> Such punishment, being customary, was not cruel then and therefore cannot legally be cruel now!

The Constitution I interpret is not living but dead or, as I prefer to put it, <u>enduring</u>. It means today not what this <u>current</u> society, much less this present Court, thinks it ought to mean in some hypothetical Absurdistan but what its words meant <u>when it was adopted in 1791!</u> Nothing more need be said! Nothing has changed! For me, therefore, the constitutionality of torturing these ungrateful foreigners does not raise a soul-wrenching question undermining our fabled hospitality. Torture of captives was <u>clearly</u> permitted at the Eighth Amendment's adoption! Any torture clearly permitted at the dawn of our country is clearly permitted today. Our great patriot Patrick Henry himself spoke approvingly of the unchanging meanings of this great amendment.[1]

What an outrageous mockery Justice Higher's dissenting opinion today makes of Alexander Hamilton's eminently reasonable expectation that the meaning of our Constitution should endure unchanged over time. Such perfidious activism reflects culpable ignorance of the rigidly dead constitutional text! Such judicial evolutionists believe not that this Court was wrong in the past but that our Constitution itself has somehow changed! Such an alteration of constitutional rigor mortis can be humored only by indulging the activist hypocrisy of reading into our Constitution evolving standards of decency, as at least three misguided decisions of this Court explicitly held before my arrival and which, of course, deserve my flipping a legal bird! (flips bird).

In my view, which is the correct one, fidelity to our Constitution requires that the chosen words of our Founders continue to enjoy today the exact same meanings given those words by those Founders nearly three centuries ago. Like the stars in the firmaments, such verbal meanings do not change. Neither does the morality of the practices they sanction. Our colonial punishment practices , including its tortures and executions even of murderous imbeciles, are thus constitutionally permissible today. [2]

These tortures, time-honored at the dawn of our nation, reflect the judicial practices of England's so-called Bloody Assizes. Decapitation, the rack, and other tortures to extort confessions were among the commonplace methods of punishment at the time of the English Bill

---

[1] It would not be an untimely culinary digression to note that the historic "Oh Henry" candy bar continues to contain down to this very day the very same delicious salty chocolate and nut mixture identical to the tasty recipe first crafted by the patriot Patrick Henry himself in his colonial kitchen and enjoyed, to this very day, on my morning constitutional.

[2] Just because today's psychology has acquired a greater understanding of mental illness than our colonial forefathers possessed does not require that such psychological advances should alter the colonial practice of executing imbeciles. The American Psychological Association, like some of my so-called esteemed colleagues on this very Court, have done legal history a disservice by expanding our Founders' knowledge of how mental illness reduces culpability. *Verbum sapienti sat est.*

of Rights when England passed its legal baton to our still-suckling democracy. These <u>accepted </u>English meanings thus also govern Eighth Amendment interpretation. [3] How, you may ask, do I know the exact meanings intended by the Founders? Because, pursuant to the doctrine of judicial notice, my daily dose of Reverend Rover's HiOctane Judicial Purgative #1 empties from my mind every legal development occurring in this country since 1791, leaving nothing left but the original bolus left by our Founders. Such is the true and only meaning of "taking a morning constitutional."

<u>Never</u> let it be said that this court – nor especially I – look lightly on the goal of impartial justice! During a private legal discussion on our recent hunting trip, I was reliably informed by Vice President Surley that this same administration, which has pledged itself to the <u>fullest</u> possible hospitality to tiny unfertilized stem cells, has yet to have whipped any stem cell to death in Guantanamo or Abu Gharib . Not a one! Furthermore, not even the Vice President or his libido would dare to engage in any waterboarding unless it was deserved! Nor has this administration as yet tortured anyone 24/7; instead it prefers, on the highest of humanitarian grounds, to offer these captives undeserved hours of rest and relaxation between beatings. Several of our unfairly maligned prison guards serving in our world-wide prisons have told me, in strict confidence, of course, that their beatings of prisoners have never exceeded a half-day at a sitting. None of these guards has been yet indicted for whipping anyone for the entire duration of a captive's life, as so deservedly befell the English traitor Oats, from whom, incidentally, our colonial Quaker Oats derives its enduring name,

---

[3]   We note, in this regard, that the American colonists faithfully followed English torture practices even to the point of executing a deserving 12 year- old girl in 1786, one Hannah Ocuish, for killing a badly - mannered 6 year- old playmate. For her and her descendents, authorities from the Fathers of the Church down to Blackstone have expressed the comforting legal principle ever so succinctly: *Memento mori.* Supposed calamities such as these tortured captives imagine receiving in our hospitable prisons at the hands of this compassionate administration provide the occasion of great virtue. As my countryman Seneca reminds us to this day, *Calamitas virtutis occasio est,* a maxim remaining <u>unchanged to this very day!</u> Indeed, calamity continues to offer a great occasion for virtue especially in today's uncertain times, providing at least a modicum of comfort to the Ocuish family, to whom I send my warmest regards

perpetuating the original puritan values of hardscrabble colonial cereal even to this day.

Any judge faithful to his oath of office would not lightly disregard such personal confidences from eyewitnesses on the very scene of these supposed tortures. My erstwhile colleagues on this Court would acquire some needed legal acumen by honoring such communications, indeed, instigating them, as I regularly do with the Vice President on our hunting trips. Just last week he informed me that the patriotic practice of waterboarding can trace its ancestry back to the Mayflower, that is, by the colonists' need to endure repeated waves of sea water to arrive on our shores !

Based on the Vice President's private communications made directly to me, in the strictest of confidence I must add, I can only conclude that the hypothetical punishments our compassionate guards inflict upon these foreign prisoners fall well short of the commonplace punishments the Mother Country inflicted on Oats and other noxious Quakers at the very dawn of our Constitution. Petitioners' monotonic claims of dog bites, pain, torture, deprivation of food and sleep, non-access to lawyers, courts and to Red Cross mediums, and denial of basic human rights pale in comparison to the Mother Country's torture inflicted on the traitorous Quaker, Oats. It ought to be of some solace to these complainants that the arrows perfectly fit their wounds !

This history coincides perfectly with what the Vice President told me in yesterday's regular phone conversation in the very privacy of my star chambers: the word "unusual" in our Eighth Amendment could hardly mean "contrary to law," he said, but must mean "such as does not occur in ordinary practice, meaning forms of punishment not regularly or customarily employed." I am persuaded and now fully concur with his view, which is hereby incorporated in this opinion as though I wrote it myself.

Based on what the Vice President has privately confided to me, only a crueler punishment differing in degree from <u>customary</u> Anglo Saxon punishments could violate our Eighth Amendment! Torture was hardly unusual at our nation's birth, having been fruitfully employed throughout our colonial history as well as that of the Mother Country[4] and still continuing today in this administration's hospitable gulags

---

[4]   Or, to use the enduring modern slang, *Alma Mater*

upon which, as was once gloriously said of the British Empire, the sun never sets.

The Crown's torture of the Quaker Oats and his unruly allies during the so-called Assizes (the Vice President sees no reason to continue to call them "bloody") reflects only the Crown's goal of silencing opposition to the unitary executive, James II, whose sovereignty our own presidency <u>directly</u> mirrors. No less is true today as we recognize the <u>kingly</u> nature and royal powers given our Chief Executive by comparison with these lesser subjects.! My countryman Syrius put it so well: *Ubi nihil vales, ibi nihil velis*: If you are valueless to begin with, you want for nothing!

These ingrates' petition falls on our judicial deaf ears. It is denied a hundredfold times! I hasten to add that this is not a one-judge decision; the Vice President, who also holds the expertise as Advocate of High Torture in this administration, assures me his libido enthusiastically concurs in it. He particularly endorses the parts about waterboarding (which he approved only in draft form, of course, not in my signed version, which will be hand-delivered to him this very day).

The foreign prisoners' compassionate torture may continue. [5] If they don't like it, let them wear bigger blindfolds. My dissenting colleagues to this opinion continue to be idiots.

Justice Scorpio re-enters his chambers and hangs his black robe on a hanger under the Latin expression <u>Vestis virum facit</u>, pleased that such a robe could constitute his humanity.

---

[5] While these prisoners' claims of pain should rightly be ignored by this compassionate administration, their bodily discomfort is nothing compared to the psychic pain being suffered by President Wondershrub whose honorary Yale D. Litt degree, I'm reliably told by the Vice President, has been rescinded as "improvidently granted." One must conclude that only an institution of learning more literate than Yale can fully appreciate our President's contributions to our mother tongue. These foreign ingrates desireous of understanding the utility of torture need only repair to Beccaria's *On Crimes and Punishments*, easily perused between beatings during free time in their cells. I am today sending each supposedly tortured petitioner an English version of this thoughtful essay plus my personal interlineated copy of Machiavelli's *The Prince*, lent to me from the Vice President's own nightstand, along with this still more eloquent opinion of mine, personally autographed and suitable for framing in their cells. *Ad astra per astra.*

6
Declaration of War Against The Royal Kingdom of Belgium

President Wondershrub emerges from the White House's Steroid Tasting Room to deliver a prime-time address to the nation on FAUX-TV. He stands at the "Mens Room" entrance to the Royal Restrooms on the South Lawn of the White House, next to advisor Reverend Rover Rasputin, Vice President Lip Surley and Secretary Brunette Brunhilde. The President wears a Captain Midnight cape, an aviator's cap, chrome sunglasses, and cowboy boots with reflector lights. He holds a Remington 45 rifle pointed at the camera. The Charwoman of the Joint Chefs serves testosterone cocktails artfully arranged on a silver platter around the hanged head of Saddam Hussein. The <u>Weakly Standard</u> Glee Club begins the program by singing "When the Cassons Go Rolling Along," with a solo by former Inspector General Johnny Ashpit.

President Wondershrub:

My fellow America, I stand before you on this lovely spring day, once again reluctantly, to announce why I have found it necessary – indeed, imperative, as I'm reminded by the Vice President – (*drops his notes, sits on the Vice President's lap and adjusts microphone*) to declare a military expedition against the sovereign Kingdom of Belgium.

The notion that we are getting ready to attack Belgium by traditional war is, course, simply ridiculous. Having said that, all options are on the table, especially a military expedition such as this. A military expedition is not exactly a conventional war but at most a distant cousin. And it's only a war if it's against a great nation like Old Europe, for example, not against a small nation like Belgium.

What has this small nation done to us?

Yesterday during a visit to the White House the Belgian ambassador to our country presented me with what he pretended was a "gift" of this small bronze statute (*demonstrating*) of a young male child relieving himself into a pool of water. He told me this gift represented a real statue standing on the Grande Place of the Belgian capital of Brussels, or Bruxelles, as the old French-speakers call it. Belgians call this statue – I apologize to use their vulgar term -- the "Manikin Pis."

Though the ambassador pretended this so-called "gift" to be a token of the friendship of the Belgian people, -- a nation, by the way, that opposed our peaceful liberation of Iraq -- Secretary Nostradamus and his intelligence services warned me that accepting this vulgar gift would resemble Helen of Troy bringing inside our walls the wooden Trojan Horse filled with Victor Hugo's toy solders brandishing their nutcrackers. As a student of military history, as rightly expected of your Commander in Chief, I know exactly both the militarist terrorism and terrorist militancy being concocted inside this so-called "gift." You would expect nothing less of your Commander in Chief.

Once I received this "gift," and without foolishly opening it, I turned it over to our security agencies for analysis. Careful investigation by the offices of the FBI, the CIA, the NSA, and the elite staff of the Homeland Security Office, and repeated readings of Frommer's and Michelin's tourist guides, unanimously confirmed that just such a hollow, bronze statue does, in fact, stand over a pool of water – "pissoir" is the Belgians' vile term -- near the Grande Place in Brussels, the capital of the country against whom I am forced to declare this military expedition. I understand that this manikin is now wearing on his torso only a Yale University T- shirt, like the one Yale gave me with my unjustly rescinded D. Litt. degree.

My fellow Americans, because mine is an open administration, dedicated to fully informing you, the American peoples, let me tell you clearly the secret reasons for today's decision to the limited extent I can disclose these secrets to mere citizens. My reasons for deciding this military expedition against the sovereign state of Belgium are as follows (*opens Sky King ring secret compartment*):

First, this statute is obscene. It violates everyone's concept of human dignity and respect for all life. One of the reasons for our invasion of Belgium lies in the scriptural need, recognized by the prophet Amos, to "make justice roll down like the waters," which means to wash away Belgium's watery vices with our cleansing waters of democracy and compassion. Furthermore, I cannot easily overlook the fact that this manikin is wearing the official T-shirt of the university that named its Linguistic College after me when it awarded me its honorary D.Litt. degree and now so cruelly has taken it all back, forcing me to take back my Captain America comics donation as well.

Furthermore, this statue is hollow. As such it is capable of holding WMD inside its belly. Indeed, our intelligence sources who have viewed this statue from unmanned drones using powerful zoom lenses at 37,000 feet surmise that this manikin contains small bronze pieces of metal inside its stomach -- "shards" is the technical military term -- with sharp edges like points on a spear, just the kind of spears held by the Swiss Guards at the Vatican. True, these pieces appear very small in a zoom lens in a plane at 37,000 feet but they can easily become larger by use of a microscope. Secretary Nostradamus informs me that many ordinary Belgians now possess microscopes. This discovery explains why we are reluctantly compelled to wiretap all Belgians suspected of possessing microscopes.

Inside the manikin's watery intestines, these small bronze "shards" can easily congregate together or "combine" exactly as conspirators do. When they do come together as a " conspiratorial combination," they resemble the pointed ends of the decorative spears held by the Vatican's Swiss Guard I just mentioned. The Swiss Guard, of course, comes from Switzerland, where Swiss knives are made. These knives, as you know, contain sharp blades similar to "shards." Switzerland has also been, as I'm sure you know, the home of Swissair, the airline company. I do not have to remind you that airlines and sharp knives figured in our 9/11 disaster. This compelling logic convinces me and my intelligence officials of the connection between the Manikin Pis and our 9/11 tragedy and the necessity for our continuing wiretapping of this unusually secretive manikin.

Even more justification exists for this peaceful military expedition. Our intelligence agencies who have been sketching the WMD in the empty white trailers in Baghdad are now convinced that Sodom himself, while married to Ms Gomorrah, and with the cooperation of the Old Belgian nation long hostile to our Iraq war, recently hid his

WMD inside this very Manikin Pis statue right in the highly populated central city of Brussels. We now have reason to believe that the pool of water circulating at the foot of this manikin may well be a disguised cooling pool for Osama bin Laden's nuclear rods. Our intelligence offices also tell me that Osama might well be hiding under these rods, just as Moses himself hid under the Pharaoh's water lilies.

There is yet another compelling reason for this invasion. This statue's vital parts are entirely naked. Recall how my administration's Justice Department, led by former Inspector General Johnny Ashpit, who is singing so beautifully here today, found this administration's values of decency to require covering the exposed breasts of the female statues posing nudely around our nation's capital. This public obscenity in Belgium demands a similar cover-up reflecting my administration's high moral standards regarding covering up any exposed epidermis of any kind. You know, of course, that even the silver tongue of former President Dioxin can be viewed only under glass in the library in San Cement, California, where I donated my inaugural oath, and no one may view his sacred tongue directly "in the flesh" except those receiving a Yale honorary D. Litt degree.

Along with Inspector General Ashpit I, too, must note my continuing displeasure that prior liberal administrations and their elites have made no effort to clothe these busomy female statutes that the CIA now confirms have been openly posing, and sometimes even suckling, for many decades throughout the capital's parks and monuments, and even, I'm told, on so-called artistic paintings in museums. I expect the CIA to make a full breast of this neglected indecency.

Back to Belgium: Nowhere in the world, not even in Old Belgium, should such a small bronze statue be allowed to relieve himself -- or itself -- in full view of the public. We have demanded that the obscene Belgian nation remove its manikin. Either it must disarm or we will. If Belgium refuses our modest request we will demand that it allow a multi-lateral cotillion under the direction of our Department of Defense to enter Belgium for the limited purpose of replacing the manikin's mocking Yale T-shirt with proper clothing and to inspect the contents of its stomach shards and, if necessary, encapsulate Osama from these filthy waters.

We will not act alone and certainly not unilaterally. While we do not consider ourselves bound by any votes of the United Nations, our administration's humanitarian goal always remains to cooperate with our allied partners in that body to get our own way on pressing clothing or stomach-related matters affecting our decisions about enemy combatants like this very manikin. I can assure you that we will not let rogue allies in Old Europe hold our nation hostile by disagreeing with my policies, as Belgium in fact has done regarding Iraq and capital punishment as well.

Regardless of any United Nations votes, it is my personal intention to do everything in my power, just as it was for Inspector General Ashpit,   to properly clothe this manikin person. Then, only if necessary, with as limited a force as compassion allows, will we seek to plug up its public leaking by unplugging its urinary water hose. Finally, only as a last resort, will we endeavor to actually seize him – or it, or her (I do not wish to appear sexist) -- and take him – or her or it-- to my oral office for thorough stomach pumping and shard de-briefing, similar to what I did in my Yale fraternity. Once these tasks are done, our goal remains simply to keep the manikin in our own country for its own protection and make him – or her, or it – available at the entrance to the Official White House Unisex Restrooms for viewing by tourists from around the world for only a modest fee, a fee that we will waive for our brave fighting men and women still being wounded in our long-completed Hunnert Day campaign in Iraq.

In addition,   though repetition is unnecessary, let me also add another further additional reason for this peaceful invasion beyond those already mentioned. We take particular offense, as all   decent persons everywhere must, at the fact that not only is this Manikin Pis statue posing nudely but also the fact that in his present location on the Brussels Grande Place his epidermis faces in the direction of our nearby American embassy with full explosure of his leaking probuscus, which is pointed threateningly at our embassy's flag.

I find this, as I'm sure all patriotic Americans do, a brazen provocation insulting   the very decency defining my administration. I hardly need to remind you of the principles of decency I solemnly set forth in my inaugural address at the tomb of the sacred tongue of President Dioxin and marbled for all time in Billy Bennett's *Book of*

Virtures. I know what I'm talking about; I too have a probuscus, though it is easily overlooked.

Last, and certainly not leastly, Secretary Nostradamus and his dedicated CIA agents have found this same manikin person to be the source of the many leaks or "leakings" to the unprepared American public of secret intelligence my administration considers so vital to our security interests. Our intelligence confirms that this male manikin person has become the true "mother of all leaks" my administration has been trying to plug up. My compassionate administration, as you know, has long been dedicated to protecting our American democracy from informative leaks of all kinds, so that our citizens remain secure in their ignorance of my administration's conduct, all in the interests of our citizens' peace of mind.

True Americorns need not be troubled by what my administration is doing about this offensive manikin. To know what this administration is doing, even in a democracy, interferes with achieving what I want to do. Leakings even by a small foreign manikin such as this breach the trust the American peoples have shown in their democratic election of me. Democracy and secrecy can coexist happily, just like a fish and a pig. To reveal what my government is doing would violate the trust you showed in voting for me to presidate. We are thus determined that this leaking must stop, whether on our soil or foreign soil, especially in any foreign pissoirs, if you'll excuse my Latin. It is for this reason that the Pentagon has termed this Belgian military expedition "Operation Leak Proof."

Accordingly, as your Commander in Chief, and as the Commander in Chief of the entire world, and mindful of what I said previously about using only minimal force, I am today reluctantly sending the 7th Fleet, the 8th Army, the Second Armored division, and the 4th and 5th Urinal Swabbers to the Belgian coastline, supported by our aircraft carrier Carebear and the nuclear battleship USS Compassion. Our goal always remains peaceful. That goal is, first, to make an amphibious landing on the very Normandy coast where William the Conquerer's famous Norse invasion ended World War II.

Once this Norman beachhead is secure, these elite units will proceed directly, with as little nuclear force as possible, to the center of Brussels, or "centre" as Old Europeans refer to it, or "Stadtmitte" as

New Europeans call it. There undercover agents from the Joint Chiefs of Staff will confront and inspect the manikin. Then, only if necessary and only on my command, they will remove any microscopically-enlarged "shards" (the technical military term) from its watery belly, once we are assured such can be done in a medically safe environment for the manikin person. If this pumping cannot be arranged on an out-patient basis, only then will I give the order to arrange for on-site CIA pumping of the contents of his, or hers, or its belly. Once that is accomplished, our CIA underwater divers will then carefully empty the nuclear cooling pool at his, or hers, or its feets. Once these tasks are accomplished, former Inspector General Emeritus Ashpit will clothe its obscene nakedness with a loincloth he personally embroidered.

Our limited military expedition shows the compassionate intentions of my administration. Recall the workplace injunction in the Book of Job to "clothe the naked." Recall, also, the lilies of the field, who toil not, neither do they spin, reminding us of the Old Testament command in the Book of DutyRoundUs that this naked manikin be clothed just as Solomon's own lily was gilded in all its glorious growth, being thereby glorified in its very gilding.

Some may interpret our actions as hostile. The world should know that we in this compassionate administration do not seek to hurt this little manikin person nor even declare it an enemy combatant, and certainly not to rendition it for waterboarding torture in any of our free world-wide prison facilities. We seek only its rendition to our own country so that we may clothe its epidermis decently, as Solomon himself would wish.

This manikin's return to its motherland remains negotiable. If a return were ever to be achieved diplomatically, (which we always prefer, of course) we would expect Belgian officials to turn its epidermis so as to remedy the vulgar insult to our flag by its exposed and leaking probuscus frontly facing our embassy five miles away.

While this manikin person resides in our country, our National Park Service will, of course, make it feel welcome as any other foreign guest in our hospitable country. The Park Service will make it available for visitors at all National Park restrooms, for only a modest fee , except, however, the citizens of this indecent Belgian nation, who will have to pay.

I know there will be criticizers of this decision. I know that. I appreciate that. I am fully mindless of that fact. I hear those voices all the time.   But, as your president, I must presidate even over criticizers of unwelcome facts no matter how true . This administration does not cherry-pick our facts; we just accept whatever decisive facts fall off the Knowledge Tree that we decide to pick up. Remember, I be the Decider. Our intentions are only peaceful, as the gentle names on the turrets of our battleship Carebear always remind us. Our ultimate goal is only to spread more democracy to the already democratic Belgian nation, the very nation Caesar's pure wife herself once described as surgically divided into three parts or "Caesarean sections," all because of foreign terrorism,   an alien terrorism not unlike that within our own country's exterior.

If you are troubled by the expense of this additional war, be assured that just as we have been able to finance the Hunnert Day Operation in Iraq by selling off only Newfoundland and Nova Scotia, we will prevail against the obscene government of Belgium by mortgaging   nothing more than Bermuda and the Bahamas and, only as a last resort, leasing out Tyre and Sidon. Texas will never be sold; no one will ever mess with Texas. No more taxes will be asked of you,   Mr. and Ms Front Porches, indeed, the market forces involved in financing this peaceful military expedition will succeed in abolishing taxes on our highest earners and oil pumpers so that we can finance this expedition with only a modest tourist tax on sunbathers at our expanding GOP lodges in Antarctica. This country is strong enough to live with a 500 year deficit and no taxes at all, at least for the next 500 years.

My fellow Americans, you can repose your entire trust in me, your Decider, in the same way you have so affectionately named me, at my suggestion, your education president, which I is, a president like Lincoln, of the people, by the people, and for all the people of the Grand Oil Party. I will take a few questions from the press. Little Sir Echo?

Q Little Sir Echo, FAUX News: Dear Beloved President, Is there some connection between crime and Belgium's leaking Manikin Pis? Is it leaking oil? I mean, Your Eminence, doesn't this public indecency suggest criminal behavior of some kind that we could do another newsworthy crime story about, in order to generate more fear in the public so you, Your Grace, could appear as a modern Messiah offering salvation from their fears?

A President Wondershrub: Excellent question. Of course, Sir Echo, there's a close connection between public indecency and crime rates. We would expect, then, that Belgium's disgusting manikin causes that obscene nation's crime rates to be much higher than ours. Greater availability of guns would help reduce Belgium's violent crime rate. Guns are the solution to fear and the best protection against injury. Look at the examples of Virginia Tech and Columbine. Or look at the example of Vice President Surley. I'd rather go hunting with him than riding with Senator Kennedy. Does a Senator shoot in the woods? Would we hear it if he did?

Q Legal Beagle News: Are you at all concerned about protecting America's civil liberties?

A President Wondershrub: When we talk about chasing down terrorists, we're talking about getting a court order before we do so. That's what our Founding Fathers and Mothers had in mind. It's important for our fellow citizens to understand, when we think of laws like the Patriot Act, that we value the entire Independence Declaration, especially its Fourth Commandment that protects a man's castles from being wiretapped, unless, of course, in my judgment national security or the Vice President's libido requires it. We expect to be as pure as Caesar's wife and all her pregnant "Caesarian sectionings". To take another example making the exact same point, Yale University has no reason, in light of my generous Captain Midnight comic book donation, to take back its honorary D.Litt. degree or to re-name the Wondershrub Linguistics College in honor of Mr Oscar Ozone. The university never did that to my daddy. That's the only reason why its president and literature department are being wiretapped.

Q Reverend Sarducci, Eternal Word TV: Some say that you are declaring war against Belgium because its government has issued a postage stamp of Karla Faye Tucker, the young woman whose execution you presided over while you were governor of Texas. Any truth to that?

A President Wondershrub: Karla Faye Tucker's case was reviewed by 13 courts and at least two lawyers after they were awakened. Inspector General Gonzo himself wrote me a detailed memo about her crime when he worked for me in Texas as my legal counsel. He tells me his memo described her horrific murder so completely that it didn't need to be read at all. As to the insensitive Belgian stamp, our intelligence agencies are even now analyzing this anti-execution stamp for any secret coded messages intended for mail recipients who may be terrorists. The fact remains that our sole reason for peacefully invading Belgium resides in the Manikin Pis leakings I just described, though we will not, of course, deliver any Belgian mail bearing that stamp, at least not until the obscene nation of Belgium agrees with my standards of decency regarding Iraq.

7

Guided Tour of the Department of Justice Building in Washington DC conducted by Inspector General Alonzo Gonzo

The Wondershrub Justice Department offers a tour for a visiting delegation of high legal officials from the newly independent states of Bosnia and Serbia. Inspector General Alonzo Gonzo addresses them as he escorts them through the Department of Justice.

Inspector General Gonzo:

My friends, or "students of justice," as I prefer to familiarly call you, I extend to each and every one of you the warmest greetings of President Wondershrub and his administration and, in particular, my Department of Justice. I am honored to be your personal tour guide today as you come to our offices to acquire from our administration some suggestions, indeed even some role models, showing how to establish in your distressed homelands a true democracy with human rights and high legal principles so difficult, I know, to achieve in your war-ravaged lands.

Let me tell you, first, some information about the American Department of Justice. This branch of the executive part of our government was previously housed in the International House of Paperwork across the street. Thanks to the Paperwork Reduction Act, we have been able to abandon those crowded offices and move here to this sacred shrine, a shrine dedicated to honor the memory of Former Inspector General Johnny Ashpit, my predecessor. The respect we have for him appears in the inscription over the entrance: "The Justice Ashpit."

This department has its main duty to collect laws and apply them in an honest and even-handed way, unlike, perhaps, the ways your past legal officials have applied your quaint third world laws. Here we not only collect all our laws but also seek to implement and interpret them equally to all our citizens, including even any non-citizens trying to gain the protection of these laws by entering our country. It is these laws that have made this administration a beacon of human rights around the world, especially in The Sudan, which sees us as its guiding model for its own legal values.

As we walk down this corridor past these stone tablets of the Ten Commandments, we first stop at a favorite exhibit of mine adjacent to my office memorializing my legal work as the chief attorney for President Wondershrub when he was Governor of Texas, before he ascended to his present royal position in the White House. My job for him then was to act as his personal acolyte . That meant that I spent a good deal of my time carefully reviewing what Texas criminal laws required him to do in capital cases, that is, cases where bad people had to be put to death. This exhibit you are now viewing consists of the photos and names of the 152 persons executed in the civilized state of Texas during his tenure there as its compassionate governor. This careful adherence to the rule of law at a minimum should give the lie to any suspicion of Texas being a third world country, like the majority of countries around the world that have abolished the death penalty, yours included.

In each of these cases he asked me, as his personal attorney, to review these death sentences and make a detailed recommendation to him about whether he should show any clemency, legal relief or other form of compassion to these 152 persons who, of course, were murderers. In each case I wrote memos, that is, technical analyses of such detail probably unusual in your less sophisticated legal systems . Based simply on the horrible facts of each case , and without the need for any legal analysis of the capital procedures of Texas, I was able to quickly recommend in each case to then-governor Wondershrub that he carry out all the capital sentences imposed on these vile criminals .

These pictures of the condemned along this Governor Wondershrub Memorial Death Row Hall (*pointing*), include old and young persons of all major sexes. During my career with Governor Wondershrub in Texas, we had nearly a 100% success rate of executions . Do you think he liked my legal work? Well, my memos described their crimes in such minute detail that in no case did then-Governor Wondershrub ever even question my recommendations for carrying out the death sentences. In fact, so well done were my descriptions of the original crimes that he saw no need to even discuss my recommendations, question me about them or, in fact, even read them.

In fact, only one person – a lower class person named Cameron Willingham -- has been found innocent of the 1991 arson deaths for which he was executed. His innocence was proven well after his execution, not before, as a result of DNA and arson forensics that no one should take seriously now that he is dead. Given its lateness – he was already pictured on the Wondershrub Memorial Death Row Hall when this DNA data came to light -- there was no reason to change his sentence. Besides, under well-recognized principles of Texas law, the double jeopardy provisions in the Magna Carta provide that no free man should be executed twice for the same offense if one execution will do, which was the case here. So our success rate on Texas executions is still well over 99% and no one is around to complain about the small remainder. You can see, then, how our scrupulous legal analyses hardly compare to the kangaroo courts your own countries have sadly experienced. You will be gratified, I know, to hear that no stem cells have ever been executed in our country, not even in Texas, during this administration.

Now, as we walk further down the hallway here, just past the Beatitudes Tablets, I want to take you to the museum where we keep models of the instruments useful for quelling insurrections in the many up-to-date prisons we operate around the world, totally free of charge, for enemy combatants and prisoners of war, including those captured in wars already happily ended and fully gilded, as in Iraq. These persons, whom we fly from prison to prison on a time-share basis, without them incurring any out-of-pocket expense, cannot be considered innocent until proven guilty, for these persons have at least once conversed by using words containing the three letters in the abbreviation "WMD", thus providing probable cause for their detention for referring to these weapons' alphabetical components . We will consider a future trial for these enemy speakers once they stop using those and the other letters of the alphabet that constitute "WMD." That simple requirement constitutes the centerpiece of the President's careful civil liberties policy for our prisons, for which, as you ought to know, he has received an honorary Yale D.Litt. degree no less.

Here in the official Department of Justice kennels, before your very eyes you can see large cages containing well-fed German Shepherd dogs that, on command , will bite these prisoners anywhere on their bodies. Take your hands away from their cages, please, if you wish to keep them! Over here you see models of our modern concrete block cells where these prisoners relax in leisure when not being bitten or beaten. These detailed pictures of these prisoners being beaten, by the way, or occasionally eaten, have been taken by our own prison guards specially trained in prison photography. Here is a photo of Islamic prisoners who, because they spoke out against their hospitable treatment by our compassionate guards, had to be forced to disrobe and climb on top of each other, to make a sort of mountain of flesh – a mountain, of course, much smaller than the ones in my home state of Texas.

Over here, on this wall next to the Sermon on the Mount plaque, hangs a copy of our beloved Declaration of Independence. We give a free copy of this Declaration to each of these foreign inmates on their arrival, so that they can learn the values our administration hopes to share with them, and indeed with the entire world, as a roadmap to human rights .

Now, as we walk further down this hallway, past the "Love One Another" inscription on the wall, I will show you the centerpiece of the Ashpit Justice Memorial, its library. This library is the special place where we keep legal books of all kinds containing the impartial laws guiding treatment of our own citizens and those of foreign countries as well. In this department we diligently try to read all these laws as best we can but, given their great number, we cannot possibly read all of them, or even most of them, and we are, of course, constrained by the Paperwork Reduction Act.

As you enter this room, please watch your step and hold onto the holy oil urns so you don't fall. You may need to light the blessed candles we've given you, because, as you note, this room has no windows. Light can impair the special legal paper on which these laws are printed. Too much reading of legal texts in a bright light also wears away the printed words. That's why legal reading in this library is limited to the hours of 2 am and 4 am of weekends, for a modest charge, except for reading Billy Bennet's *Book of Virtures*, which can be read by administration officials free of library charges at any time, as a guide for compassionate and, indeed, virtuous legal interpretation.

Our laws are contained entirely in this single bookcase on the far wall. Our other three walls, you will note, display life-size portraits of my predecessors and role models in this office, the Grand Inspector Robespierre, Grand Inquisitor Torquemada, and of course, my immediate predecessor, former Inspector General Johnny Ashpit, whose goals I aspire to imitate myself. To make room for these role model portraits we had to remove pictures of nine Justice Department attorneys from these walls who fell short of the political values of the Wondershrub administration, such as devotion to capital punishment.

You may be edified to know that when he first assumed his high position as Inspector General, my predecessor, Inspector Ashpit, had himself anointed with sacred Balsamic Cooking Oil, just like King David of the Old Testament. His anointing reflects his respect for the inviolability of all human life, as shown by his calling to clothe the naked bosoms of females posing in statues and portraits around this city and his current international mission to clothe the naked David statue in Florence, Italy and the obscene hyena of the Manikin Pis statute in Brussels, Belgium. Mr Willingham, while he was alive, escaped his attention because he was not posing nudely on the Texas Death Row and his breasts were nearly fully covered by execution protocols.

Note, now, that this bookcase has many shelves, showing the multiplicity of laws in our country. Indeed, ours is a country of laws, as you should know, not of men. The laws have usually been arranged on these shelves in a hierarchy, with the most universal federal laws like international treaties on the top shelf, followed on the lower shelves by laws enacted by Congress, followed further down by state laws. At the very top, above all the others, is the glass-enclosed shelf holding the orders signed by the President himself.

On the shelf just below the signing orders, you see the treaties our nation has signed with foreign countries. These include the Vienna Convention and the Geneva Convention. We put these on a high shelf because, as treaties, they enjoy the greatest force of law in our land after presidential signing statements, binding not only the federal government but also our individual states, except for Texas, my home state, a very humane place, so unlike your quaint countries. On these shelves you would have recently found the many adverse decisions of the International Court of Justice in The Hague, just north of the indecent Belgian country. We were once bound by the Vienna Convention because we signed it, but the ink has totally dried now. We once also became bound by the many decisions of the InterAmerican Court of Human Rights and the Court of the Organization of American States, of which we are also a proud member. Its recent adverse decisions, however, do not meet our exacting legal standards so we have accordingly had to remove them as well.

I know the vast expanse of these laws in just one bookcase on one wall of an otherwise empty law library must be a great surprise to you coming, as you do,   from your war-torn countries so lacking in up-to-date law libraries. Your own legislatures , I know, have not enjoyed the luxury of enacting many laws or implementing any human rights standards because your countries have been so involved in wars. We in this peace-loving administration are very proud of our own laws, for, as I may have mentioned, this administration enjoys the proud habit of saying that we are a country of laws, not of men.

Let me share with you, as aspiring professionals in the legal and human rights fields, one of our own most pressing problems for whatever help or guidance it may be to you.   The presidential signing orders here are overflowing. Since he took office the President has issued 750 signing orders about laws passed by Congress that he has decided he will not enforce because he finds them unconstitutional. You can appreciate how efficient these signing orders are in saving this administration the time and costs of constitutional litigation over legislation so unnecessary in a democracy such as ours.   As we acquire more and more of these presidential signing statements telling us how to ignore laws passed by our Congress, we must, of course, find room in the bookcase to store them properly. In our American democracy presidential signing statements enjoy much greater force than the quaint laws passed by our elected Congress.

Because space is limited on this bookcase, the only way we can make room requires removing the treaties and court decisions previously placed on the top shelf to make space for the President's many signing statements. We do not do this lightly but only after the same careful consideration this administration gave to the decision to invade Iraq . The need to make space for presidential signing statements has recently required us to remove article 36 on consular access from the Vienna Convention, the long provisions of the quaint Geneva Convention dealing with treatment of prisoners of war, as well as all acts of Congress and Supreme Court decisions prior to this administration.

You may well ask, What is the legal effect of moving these documents around in our legal bookcase ? Let me take the simple prisoner example. Not being in a declared war, of course, means that these legal standards of treaties like the Geneva and Vienna Conventions no longer apply to us, though they do apply to other nations who, like us, signed these treaties, like for example The Sudan. The ink of our signatures is now completely dried out . Besides, there is no longer room on our shelves for these treaties, so we have had to shred them into smaller pieces in the basement of the International House of Paperwork. These pieces of paper remain there in large bins for research work by eminent judges from our Supreme Court, such as my mentor, Justice Humpty Dumpty, who is currently engaged in putting these shreds back together again.

You may well wonder what happens to these other truly superfluous laws, like these dealing with international courts or treaties with foreign governments, when we remove them from our bookcase? What you see over here across the hall in this huge sanctuary is this large shredder placed in the center of the altar where these superfluous legal documents, after a short farewell prayer, are quickly unbound, blessed and cut neatly into bite-sized shreds. Not surprisingly, we call this machine "The Justice Shredder." Being environmentally sensitive -- we care as much about the environment as about the law --we do not haphazardly discard these shreddings. Instead, after sprinkling them with blessed oils, we bag them as mulch for our creative Environmental Protection

Agency, which sells them as chocolate-covered compost to feed prisoners holiday meals in our world-wide prisons.

Let me share with you, finally, a personal example of how seriously this administration views its legal duties. Just yesterday our President appointed me to chair a committee of lawyers from the Federalist Society, hand picked by Vice President Lip Surley, after consultation with Justice Antediluvian Scorpio, to review key provisions of our Declaration of Independence. This committee will be studying this historic document not only in the context of the day when it was first written but also in light of the terror threats facing our nation today, to decide if some or all of its provisions have become outmoded. I suspect we will find no problems with the "life, liberty and pursuit of happiness" language. However, certain other sections of the Declaration are troublesome, especially those dealing with "consent of the governed." That language seems to foster unpatriotic thoughts, such as the free thinking anarchy your countries of Old Europe have so sadly experienced. The part about civil liberties appears redundant as well, because we already enjoy more civil liberties in this country than we can use.

Once our work is complete, the President will issue a new signing statement indicating how much of the original Declaration he will recognize and what parts he will ignore as unconstitutional. That signing statement will then sit on the honored top shelf in our bookcase next to the Declaration, under glass, of course.

Seeing that you have no questions, I will bring some closure to our pleasant dialogue. I have greatly enjoyed meeting you and sharing with you, in this equal give-and-take, the high ideals guiding this administration's groundbreaking approach to legal values. My hope is that, as you return to your own distressed countries, you will look across the seas with admiration at the Wondershrub Administration's record of human rights as a beacon for implementing some small part of these values in your impoverished lands, just as The Sudan has done.

Let me give each of you, as you leave, a copy of our department's annual Human Rights Report. Our department and the state department issue this detailed report every year. It criticizes the human rights failings of most other countries of the world, including yours. This big volume should give you some idea of the high standards our administration holds for spreading human rights among all other nations in the world that, like yours, fall short of the lofty principles we hold so dear in this administration.

As you prepare to leave the hallowed halls of this Justice Ashpit, I bless you, my students, and sprinkle you with these sacred Hallibuttox oils (*sprinkles oil*) as an absolution from your many sins. I encourage your leaders to follow our administration's high ideals in your pursuit of justice. We wish you all the best in trying to approximate, even in small part, the noble goals of this administration and to richly experience, as Amos says in our Scriptures , "Justice rolling down like waters".

As you leave this sacred temple, out of respect for former Inspector General Ashpit, we ask you women visitors to fully cover your boobs .

8

Swearing-in of the Sturgeon General and Dedication of Glacier Memorial National Park, Logan Pass, Montana.

Secretary Windy of the Department of the Inferior stands with the Sturgeon General of the Environmental Protection Agency on a psychedelic - painted stage surrounded by luxury loge boxes carved into boulders abutting Logan Pass, at the summit of the Going to the Sun Road in the center of Glacier National Park.

Secretary Windy:

I am just so honored, ladies and gentlemen, truck drivers, and you hundreds of snowmobilers, to welcome you all here on this lovely spring day to Glacier National Park for this special opportunity for bonding with nature and witnessing the swearing-in our administration's new Sturgeon General. We are fortunate to have with us today the Sturgeon General-designate of the Environmental Protection Agency, along with the troupe of tumblers from his office who just entertained you. A special round of applause for all these talented EPA tumblers ! (*applause*)

I also wish to extend another special welcome to the many of you off-road four-wheelers and "hogs" who have driven here cross-country right to the heart of this majestic park by blazing your own trails through the virgin forest . A special welcome, too, to the many drivers of the 18-wheelers who maneuvered their rigs so professionally up the narrow hiking trails leading to this majestic summit. We are also honored to host today the finalists of the NASCAR competition whose winner will be decided right here later today .

I now will first ask the Sturgeon General to come forward and repeat the Hippocratic Oath after me:

"By the gods Zeus and Apollo, I do swear on these porcine entrails of mind-numbering wurst, to fully perform my duties as the nation's medical and veterinary doctor in this administration to the best of my ability under the best of service to President Wondershrub, so as to further his political goals. To these ends, by Zeus and his lesser gods and goddesses, I solemnly swear that any health-related speeches I deliver in this office will favorably mention the name of President Wondershrub at least three times on each page. Further, I hereby swear, on the innards of the great Goose and Geese and Moose and Meese formerly living on this site, to attribute to him rather than to my office any medical discoveries made by any physicians, surgeons or veterinarians occurring during my medical services for this nation.

By all the Vestal Virgins of our National Park System, of any sex whatsoever, I further solemnly swear by Hippocrates, and on the bowels of the former Great Bears of this Glacier Park, that I will make only medical discoveries and recommendations that have been pre-approved by President Wondershrub, MD, (*honoris causa*), and by the druggists in the Office of Political Affairs of the Department of Health Services and seconded by the Head of the Veterinary Office of the National Park Service.

May Dionysius, Hippocrates, and the compassionate gods of anesthesia confer blessings on me and my medical research, to the greater honor and glory of President Wondershrub, MD, DVM (*honoris causa*) whose medical and veterinary expertise I am so honored to partake and expand ." (*applause*)

Secretary Windy: Congratulations to you on your oath of office, Doctor, and welcome to the high office of Sturgeon General. We know your loyalty will be richly rewarded by your devoted service to the healing arts of this administration, especially its compassionate use of anesthesia.

We have several additional reasons for this public convocation here at Glacier. National Park. Let me first ask our new Sturgeon General to take the microphone with an explanation of these reasons.

Sturgeon General: Thank you, Madame Secretary. Yes, indeed, we are here for several wonderful outdoor events today in this lovely park, so rich in history and tradition and so healthy for mind and body. My own personal reason for coming to this noble site, as you might suspect, deals with our lovely waters . For several years now since this administration took office, the waters of Lake McDonald and its tributaries have been filling up with debris from animal carcasses, forest fire equipment, gasoline and oil from motor boats, and debris and offal left by campers, heavy rigs and snowmobilers using the park's new Snowmobile Refuge Center and Interstate Truck Stop. Over the course of years this debris has accumulated in large quantities in the park's parking lots, lube pits , and speedboat ramps, as well as on the banks and bottoms of our lakes and rivers. The result is that fish of all kinds, including the sturgeon of my namesake, have been dying off at an alarming rate.

After careful environmental studies, my office has determined that the most cost-effective remedy for these problems involves removing all fish and other water creatures, both living and dead, from all bodies of water in this park, so that these creatures no longer have to drink or even swim in these foul waters Removing these sturgeon, fish, turtles, beavers and other aquatic beings will benefit the truckers, snowmobilers, campers, and fast-fooders who eat, camp and defecate on these lovely shorelines, and wash, sandblast, lubricate, paint and pin-stripe their vehicles at the Glacier Mobile Home Parks, as they admire the majestic beauty here while listening to their boomboxes and watching famous events like today's NASCAR finals on the park's big-screen TVs .

Secretary Windy of the Department of the Inferior will describe for you what we propose to do regarding these threatened species.

Secretary Windy: Yes, thank you so much, General. It is true that both our offices have been increasingly concerned about the medical and environmental threats to the wonderful flora and fauna as well as to the health of animals living in this majestic park. To solve these problems we are announcing an innovative approach that, if successful here, this administration will implement in all our other beautiful national parks.

The fish and animal problems described by the Sturgeon General require us to devise a way to alleviate the suffering of these beings as well as to stop their defiling of the park's overcrowded parking lots by their inconvenient deaths and dyings. Here is our administration's plan. For those water creatures still alive, our dedicated National Park Rangers will collect them from all the park's waterways and roads and shorelines and then load them in the dumpsters of the red, white and blue 24- wheelers you see parked around you right here at Logan Pass. Uniformed rangers will drive these trucks throughout the park collecting any additional dying or useless animals or fish, such as those that collide with hurrying park vehicles. These big rigs, you'll note, have many large windows so the creatures inside, if still alive, can easily look outside to admire the beauty of their home as they are escorted out of it.

Our park rangers will then drive their trucks across the beautiful northern and western regions of our country to the enchanting Pacific coast, where they will dump their precious cargo as gently as possible over the awesome cliffs at Big Sur, California, directly into the Pacific Ocean. There, those animals, such as the fresh-water fish, beaver, otter, muskrat, and turtles that used to live here in the oily waters of this park, will be given the opportunity to adapt to the challenges of salt water life. A chaplain from the faith-based office in the Environmental Protection Agency will be on duty to administer any last rites to any still living creatures who may be needing spiritual comfort, and the Sturgeon General himself will be present to administer any needed anesthesia or euthanasia.

We will repeat this procedure until all these majestic creatures are fully removed from the park's waterways. We will follow the same practice for any remaining bear or elk or moose roadkill hit by our industrious truckers or, for example, by boat drivers during the park's annual speedboat competitions. For any creatures like the dying sturgeon on the shores of Lake McDonald or large animals like elk and deer that cannot be accommodated in these 18 wheelers or in the freight cars on the park's new lumber rail lines, we are today proudly inaugurating a new pipeline debris collection system to address the problem of these troublesome animals. Our dedicated National Park Rangers will collect the dead and dying carcasses of these large creatures, and as gently as possible, with the compassion characterizing this administration, will carefully dump their bodies directly into the large Y-shaped funnels at the pipeline openings you see here at Logan Pass.

The arms of these funnels lead into the large glass pipeline you see over here (*demonstrating*). This glass pipeline, which is wholly above ground for unimpeded public viewing – this administration prides itself on its open pipeline policy! -- is one of several carrying the melting waters of the remaining glaciers in this park to drought-stricken regions of our lower 50 states, such as Florida, Mississippi, Louisiana, Texas, Oklahoma, Arkansas, New Mexico, Arizona and California. These states all need more water to help extinguish the forest and grass fires plaguing them over the past decades of what Mr Oscar Ozone calls "extended drought," which we know, of course, to be such an entertaining fiction, hardly deserving his Oscar award .

You may well ask, how does this funnel and pipeline system work? Well, thanks to your reduced tax dollars, and the dedicated work of these park rangers so devoted to protecting our beautiful national parks, it works like this: Every hour of the day these rangers drive along this beautiful park's expressways in 50- ton garbage trucks where they collect these dead or dying animals injured or killed by expressway traffic or caught in our official red-white-and- blue traps . Park rangers directly transport these beings to this large Y-shaped funnel and dump them gently into the crotch where the pipeline sections join together. At that junction a large noiseless vacuum suctions these unwanted beings forward into a series of rendering devices – jackhammers, sludgehammers, pistons, pilings, and the rotating blades we call "slicers" and "separaters" – that cut and pulverize the animal flesh and bones into tiny particles.

These tiny corporeal particles travel in a slurry into this valve right over there (*demonstrating*) where they are squeezed under thousand pound weights to extract high grade oil from their carcasses. This animal oil flows forward in this other big glass pipeline over here (*demonstrating with pointer*) to be sold on the open oil market to such oil companies as, for example, Hallibuttox and its subsidiaries, after fair bidding of course. The remaining debris – the unusable and dried corporeal residue -- surges forward in these pipelines with the help of the rushing waters flowing from the melting glaciers, such as those melting right here where we're standing today! Isn't that exciting! These enriched waters carry this oil-free body debris directly to this pipeline exit valve here (*demonstrating*), where the contents are compressed again under thousand pound weights to form the richest animal compost you can imagine!

What do we do with this compost? you may rightly ask. For this administration's hard-working entrepreneurs nothing at all is lost! This pipeline's second valve carries the compost at a very cost effective price across the country, right down to Washington DC. Pipeline controls in the South Lawn of the White House allow the President or the Vice President to merely press a button to divert the fresh compost directly onto the trees, bushes, and flowering plants around government buildings that make our capital such a verdant garden for residents and visitors alike to admire. Under our generous rendition policies, any excess compost is decorated with fish skins, to be given on holidays to residents enrolled in our world-wide time-share prisons.

I remember fondly coming to this park as a child when many terribly cold snow-capped glaciers dominated the horizon at all times of the year. I can even remember when the world's North and South Poles had ugly polar ice instead of the asphalt highways and suburban streets our administration is now constructing there. The departure of the polar ice caps and the melting of the glaciers formerly defiling this park allow us to re-establish direct contact with the earth without any icy intermediary.

One unique advantage for you GOP consumers in the audience is the opportunity to sunbathe now on the administration's Glacier Memorial Beaches right at the North and South Poles. As another benefit, our administration will allow you to enjoy these glacier waters at the coin-operated glacier water fountains the Environmental Protection Agency is now installing throughout our nation's capital. These glacier water fountains allow us all to remember those rugged frontier days when our pioneering forefathers had to trek over ugly snow-capped glaciers without the comfort of glacier drinking water and without direct contact with the soil beneath their feet!

Given these changes here, I am officially renaming this lovely park the "Glacier Memorial National Park," so that we never forget how it used to look before we improved it by marketing its icy glacier waters for parched areas of our country, indeed, for the thirsty world at large, for only a modest cost to consumers.

Before we return to our cars, trucks, snowmobiles, and 18- wheelers to join the crowds assembling for the NASCAR finals , let me extend to you my heartfelt thanks for sharing this administration's values about our beautiful environment. This is a value shared, of course, by our NASCAR racers as well. I am especially excited to tell you today that this year's race ought to be one of the fastest because of the newly completed ten-lane race course connecting this Park's east and west lodges . What a thrilling course for NASCAR racers to drive! And no glaciers to slide on! Let's all hope that our visitors get to see them set a new speed record today! Let's watch, too, to see if our uniformed NRA sharpshooters have to take down any remaining stray elk or deer that wander onto the race track before they disturb our racers.

Now, as you prepare to blaze your own trails through the forest, please take your song sheets and join with me and our new Sturgeon General and the entire chorale of the Environmental Protection Agency in signing "America the Beautiful." We'll do a repeat of that verse about "purple mountain majesty." For any latecomers in the crowd who lack song sheets, the lyrics appear on the electronic billboards on the peaks around you! As you leave, be sure not to litter!

9
Press Conference in the White House Disco Room

Secretary of State Brunette Brunhilde conducts the press conference in the Cosmetic Dressing Room Vestibule to the Disco Room, with the assistance of Press Secretary Whiteout and his musical assistant Soothing Platter, who stands at the music console. Platter plays a recording of Don McLean's "Bye, Bye American Pie".

Platter: Secretary Whitehout will have a few announcements in just a moment. Let me first adjust the strobe lights and hang one more poster behind the podium showing us winning the global war on terrorism. (*adjusts lights and hangs poster*).

Secretary Brunhilde :

I will begin with the less upsetting news. Unnamed high government sources in our Department of Surrogate Intelligence have just notified the office of Press Secretary Whiteout that President Wondershrub landed safely today on the coast of Belgium, not far from the site of the Normandy Invasion that ended World War II. The President waded ashore in his Captain America combat fatigues through high seas, with Field Marshall Emeritus Rumpelstilskin at his side, along with an advance unit of our elite Valkries.

When the President's landing party came ashore on the Belgian coast, he first waved a cheery hello to Belgian sunbathers nearby and thanked them for their support of his invasion. He then re-christened the beach "Democracy Shore" to commemorate this administration's democracy goals motivating his signing statements as well as inspiring all his military operations, including those against democratic countries such as Belgium. The President then strode to a specially erected podium on the historic beach. There he gave a brief welcome to tourists wandering the sand dunes and beachcombers collecting sea shells. In this major speech, he declared offensive operations in Belgium's Grande Place to be officially ended even before they began. He then planted a gilded lily in the beach. Former Inspector General Ashpit then sang for the troops the official sending-forth song, "On Eagles Wings."

The President's unannounced trip to Belgium intended in part to shore up the Valkries' morale as they prepared to struggle against expected resistance in the narrow and winding streets approaching the Manikin Pis statue in Brussels' Grande Place. That is the background of today's grim events. Secretary Whiteout, I know you have some more somber news to add .

Secretary Whiteout: Yes, unfortunately I do. My news is somber indeed. As you know the President waded ashore in his military fatigues on the Norman coast earlier today not only to accompany the advance units of our heroic Valkries but also to show his desire to personally serve his country in uniform during wartime in the spirit of his role models Gene Autry, Roy Rogers and Tom Mix. Events unfortunately have not turned out as he wished.

Madam Secretary, my eyes are tearing -- do you wish to continue with the somber news?

Secretary Brunhilde: Indeed, the news is so tragic. The President remained on the invasion beach for several hours awaiting the arrival of Belgian schoolchildren who were expected to assemble to offer him *pommes de terre* and to place bracelets of Belgian chocolates around his neck. When they did not appear, he strolled along the boardwalks in Ostende shaking hands with shopkeepers and tourists and handing out Texas Ranger insignia to small children. He then patiently stood at the crest of the highest sand dune awaiting the cheers of the townspeople who, you would expect, would be overjoyed at their imminent liberation from their obscene Manikin Pis. Unfortunately these welcoming parties failed to materialize.

When these events did not occur, the President returned to his troops. He resolutely advanced forward through the Belgian lowlands with the elite Valkries leading the way. He was accompanied by the tactical support of the Second Decency Brigade and the Fifth Democratic Tank Divisions, all following the lead blazed by the White House Loincloth Battalion. The President served as the rear guard to protect these troops from any rear-end salvos. The units marched over rugged cornfields and past ancient castles containing snipers and insurgents disguised as ordinary husbands and wives eating their dinners at military bunkers cleverly disguised as conventional "dining room tables." The President decided – that is his job, of course-- that these suspicious so-called "spouses" should be placed under arrest for interrogation and that their disguised "dining room tables" be dismantled and searched for hidden copies of offensive Belgian postage stamps.

The President then disembarked from his stretch limo for a photo-op at the outskirts of Brussels, the capital of Old Europe that, up to now, has somehow failed to see the wisdom of his campaigns for decency and compassion. From there he marched, with the Loincloth Battalion in the lead, directly into the so-called "centre" or "Stadtmitte" of downtown Brussels. He struggled courageously over rough cobblestones against combative throngs of shoppers, waves of tourists, and hordes of sightseers mingling around the Grande Place. Their shopping bags and cameras interfered substantially with his military maneuvers.

As the President was advancing inch- by- inch along the thronged streets near the Grande Place, struggling against shoppers pushing against him from all sides but not recognizing him in his flight jacket and cowboy boots, he instructed the commander of the Valkries to search heavily laden shoppers and tourists due to confirmed intelligence reports, received in his Sky King Ring's Secret Compartment, that their shopping bags might be carrying 500 pound bunker buster bombs.

The President swiftly approached and confronted the obscene manikin. The President placed it under arrest. It said nothing in its defense and wisely offered no resistance. Then the President began to remove it from its pedestal by use of his military blowtorch. His goal was merely to remove the manikin and take it to the nearby amphibious portable dressing room carried by the Valkries, so that former Inspector General Ashpit could clothe its epidermis with an anointed loincloth

At that moment, without even permitting him to inspect the manikin's water pools hiding nuclear cooling rods, Belgian secret police, brazenly disguised as tourists, emerged from hiding places behind the statue, charged President Wondershrub, captured him and took him away in vehicles of the Belgian Mental Health Brigade . Their vehicles, we understand, bore the very Manikin Pis insignia the President and indeed all patriotic Americans find so offensive. These insurgents made no effort to salvage his blowtorch or the dressing room.

This news, of course, comes as a profound source of shock and awe to all patriotic Americans who continue to repose their total trust in him as their visionary Commander in Chief and World Decider.

Soothing Platter changes the music to "We All Live in a Yellow Submarine."

Secretary Brunhilde pauses to wipe her eye, then continues: We have been able to gain information about the President via the good diplomatic services of The Sudan, one of the countries with whom we continue to have good relations. Indeed, we have no better foreign friend than The Sudan. Sudanese diplomats tell us that President Wondershrub is being held incommunicado in a dank prison in an unknown location off the coast of Belgium without any charges lodged against him. Despite Belgium's signature on the Vienna Convention he is being denied communication with Red Cross officials, attorneys, consular officials, courts and the outside world. He is subjected to daily whippings and deprived of food, sleep, recreation, and comic books. We have been told that he has been repeatedly bitten by rabid Islamic dogs for his failure to divulge any information coherently.

His captors have also photographed him naked and forced him to perform gay sex acts before TV cameras, even to the point of soiling his person. Supposedly an insulting neon statute of the unclothed Manikin Pis flashes on- and- off over the toilet in his cell. We have tried to arrange access for him to the nearest American consular officials, but we have been informed that the Vienna Convention no longer applies to him because of its dry ink. We have learned that he is also being subjected to psychiatric examinations against his will and being force-fed Reverend Rasputin's entire product line of oily purgatives.

Soothing Platter walks to a 1950s jute box, changes music to Johnny Ray's "My Heart Cries for You."

Secretary Brunhilde: Through the good services of The Sudan we have lodged protests with the Belgian ambassador, the United Nations, and the International Court of Justice, as well as the European Court of Human Rights in Straussbourg. I will continue to inform you as more presidential indignities are reported to us.

Secretary Whiteout: We can take a few questions. Little Sir Echo.

Q Little Sir Echo, FAUX NEWS: Is our beloved President Wondershrub in any pain? How can we help His Holiness in this, his hour of need? Can we keep our studios in his White House bedroom while he's away so we can continue to be fair and balanced?.

A Secretary Brunhilde: We are working through diplomatic channels with The Sudan as we speak. We are imploring its embassy in Brussels to pressure his insurgent captors to reduce his torture but to no avail as yet. As to the President's bedroom, you may continue to keep your studios there, of course,   but should not disturb his comics on the nightstand nor the contents of the adjoining Steroid Tasting Room.

Q Ms Prober, Investigative News Now: Does your office have any intention to release pictures of the President shaking hands and talking with convicted lobbyist Jack Abramhoff, the same who has visited Belgium as part of his lobbying efforts?

A Secretary Brunhilde: Jesus didn't have his picture taken with Judas except at the Last Supper table. The President is captive in Belgium. He could hardy take pictures at a solemn time like this. Instead his own naked picture taken by his Belgian captives has been leaked to international news outlets , a leaking that, of course, we find especially offensive to this administration's high standards of decency. Former Inspector General Ashpit is particularly concerned not only at the kidnapping but also at the President's nude hyena.

Q Bear Blitzkrieg, CANNED NEWS: Is there any connection between this treatment of the President and global warming?

A Secretary Brunhilde: Let me pass that question to Secretary Windy from the Department of the Inferior.

Secretary Windy: There is only an indirect connection. As you may know, before he left to conduct the Norman invasion, the President signed an executive order to resolve global warming scares once and for all. To the extent they can be made public, the details of that order provide for above-ground pipelines to carry the melting waters of the arctic glaciers to the supposedly dry southwest of our country, to extinguish the spreading fires in Oklahoma, Texas, Colorado, New Mexico, California and Arizona. The water travels in Hallibuttox pipelines directly under the Vice President's Central Pipeline Controls located on the South Lawn of the White House. This order should squelch, once and for all, any of Mr Ozone's liberal speculation about this administration's indifference to any drought said to be caused by the greenhouse gasses ballyhooed by godless climatologists. We know it's not the heat but the humility.

The rising glacier waters are siphoned off these pipelines and can be piped directly into the drought areas of friendly countries in the same way. The levees around Washington DC on the Potomic are expected to hold against the rising waters. Belgium is apparently annoyed that this same executive order does not channel any melting glacier waters to that parched country. Belgium and other low countries in Old Europe claim they are suffering from imaginary global warming. Belgium's climate concerns have not yet prompted it to take necessary steps against the threatening Manikin Pis or to rescind its offensive Karla Faye Tucker postal stamp criticizing our capital punishment. Belgian annoyance may explain the waterboarding tortures being inflicted on the President in his illegal captivity.

Q Mr Beaglehead of Legal News: Will the Red Cross be given access to the President's prison cell?

A: SecretaryWhiteout: We are trying our best to establish contact between the President and our consular officials, but, as you may know, our administration has recently withdrawn from the Vienna Convention on consular relations. Belgium is opposed to providing the President access to live Red Cross officials as well as access to our consular officials or even to an attorney or to a court or a psychiatrist of his choice. Though he is held captive, he has yet to be charged with any crime. We will continue to demand that Belgium provide him with these basic rights considered universal among all civilized countries of the world outside our own borders. Vice President Lip Surley will assume the duties of the President in his absence.

Q Legal Beagle: About the Belgian insurgency, is it increasing or diminishing?

A Secretary Whiteout: The Vice President assures us that the Belgian insurgency now writhes in its last throes, just as in the country of Iraq. Field Marshall Rumpelstilskin Emeritus also said as much in his regular guest commentary on FAUX MILITARY NEWS yesterday.

Q Ms Horned Rim, Elite Liberal TV: Speaking of the Vice President, will he be happier in the Oval Office than where he was? Why does he always have that deformation on his lips as though he's in pain or got something stuck in his jaw?

A Soothing Platter: The Vice President suffers from an undiagnosed hoof and mouth condition that causes his lips to grimace in constant pain. Your question is totally out of line. Are you taking one of Reverend Rasputin's purgatives?

Q Ms Pet Sitter, Liberal Animal Rights News: Rumors are that he has bird flu – any truth to that? Or mad cow disease? Or fatal Hallitosis? Is his jaw receiving Hallibotox treatments?

A Secretary Whiteout: Your questions are completely out of line. Vice President Surley's oral diagnosis is, as you should expect, a private matter between him and his God, or occasionally for his team of plastic surgeons. The Vice President is a very private person who prefers that no one know anything about him. That's why our government has exempted him from any personal wiretapping or communication with the citizenry . I can only tell you that hundreds of expert plastic surgeons have worked with him, unsuccessfully, on his lip malfunction. Hallibotox injections have been tried but failed . It is grossly impolite to suggest, as you do, that his mouth appears to be in a permanent sneer. Take a purgative!

Q: Bear Blitzkreig, CANNED NEWS; When will we see Darth Vader, er, I mean the Vice President, or shake his hand? Does his desire for privacy extend to other Americans, like those he wants to wiretap?

A: Soothing Platter: He is expected to emerge for his annual press conference on Groundhog Day. As to shaking hands, the Vice President does not like bodily contact of any kind. He has a very private body, as you should know from his opposition to conversing in public, unless of course these conversations involve unilateral rather than bilateral talking. While he occupies the Oval Office Vice President Surley will, of course, constitute a fourth branch of government apart from the executive branch, because our system of checks and balances now requires that, as President Pro Tem, he legislate, prosecute, and implement laws in unitary ways that transcend the limited confines of each of these branches.

You're overlooking the important news of the day about the terrible plight of our beloved President.

Q Ike Ironic, Cable Caper TV: Yes, of course, back to the Headline News Alert! Does the administration see any conflict between the way Belgium is treating President Wondershrub and our nation's prison practices in Guantanamo and Abu Gharib?

A Secretary Whiteout: The music has ended now, so this press conference is over. Thank you all for your trust in the unnamed high government sources in this administration. We look forward to talking with you again, unless, of course, we decide we won't.

10

FAUX NEWS Psychiatric Alert!

Really Unruly: This is Really Unruly speaking to you directly from our studios in the presidential bedroom on the top floor of the White House, with a FAUX – NEWS PSYCHIATRIC ALERT!

Our studios have just received what purports to be a bona fide psychiatric report of President Wondershrub! Unnamed sources in the Belgian government apparently permitted this private report to be generated by the International Red Cross. Apparently it was intended to be kept secret except to the Red Cross out of compassion for the President. Now, thanks to our underground sources, and our cable news cooperation with our government's wiretapping of the International Red Cross, we have acquired exclusive access to this secret report about our President.

We are pleased to present to you our fair and balanced FAUX Psychiatric Expert, Dr Geepak Goopooh. Dr Goopooh.

Dr Goopooh:

Yes, that's correct, Really. I have a copy of the report right here. Apparently the Belgian government was concerned over President Wondershrub's behavior while incarcerated and receiving torture, so they permitted the Red Cross to hire a team of Old European psychiatrists to interview the President, look into his background, and work up this report as a guide for their prison treatment of him. Thanks to the Vice President's world-wide wiretapping services, we have been able to acquire a firsthand copy of the President's psychiatric report directly from the wiretap source. Its ink is not yet dry.

I propose to read our viewers the unvarnished report, and then I'll be happy to answer any questions relating to it.

The report begins by noting a deep psychological dynamic swirling around the President's feelings of inadequacy, focused in good part on his ambivalent relationship with his father. The terms "success" and "failure" consume his thoughts and dictate the rhetoric he uses in his public pronouncements. The phrases "success" and "stay the course" are necessary for the survival of his wounded psyche.

From the time he was a boy President Wondershrub felt, by comparison with his father, that he was an abject failure. His school reports show a young man harboring continuous and obsessive attempts to emulate his bigger-than-life father, obtain his approval, and escape from the hostile forces he came to associate with Yale University – its liberalism, its elitism, its educational requirements, its many library books without pictures. This partly explains his seeming vindication when Yale presented him with an honorary D. Litt. degree and named its Linguistics College, temporarily, in his honor.

These traits appear in some of his political campaigns. During his second campaign for governor of Texas, in a spontaneous outburst, he told a reporter: "It's hard to believe but …I don't have to worry about being my father's son. Maybe it's a result of being confident. I'm not sure how the psychoanalysts will analyze it, but I'm not worried about it. I'm really not. I'm a free guy."

Part of the ambivalence toward his father involves resentment at what his father was able to accomplish on the world stage. His father thereby became an overpowering role model for the son. As he entered politics, the son felt he had to prove himself to his father and receive his approval. The best way of doing so was to outdo his father as president, thus generating a dueling father-son presidency battle. This compulsion appears in his decision to re-fight his father's war against Iraq, to win it (he thought his father failed to do so) and to achieve the ultimate war trophy of capturing Saddam Hussein. By taking Baghdad, capturing Saddam, putting his head on a platter like John the Baptist, and imposing his own style of democracy on the Iraqi people, President Wondershrub estimated he could emulate his father, outdo him, and show his contempt for him all at once, sort of like a Playboy of the Western World.

We have indications in his behavior of this father-son tension. Some are especially noteworthy:

- when he took office as president, his took the oath at the tomb of the silver tongue of former President Dioxin to show how he could reach a level of maturity and eloquence surpassing his wimpish father.
- when he received the Yale honorary D. Litt degree in linguistics for his contributions to the English language, he felt that his triumph over his father was so complete that it had been publicly recognized by his receipt of an honor never given his father. Yale's decision to rescind the degree and to re-name its Wondershrub Linguistic College restored his prior feelings of inadequacy, failure and submission .
- the 9/11 disaster was too great for him to comprehend. As the world knows, when the news came to him, he sat stunned for seven minutes in a crowd of school children. He disappeared for three days, descending into a kind of hell of his own making, before resurrecting himself before the American people wielding a bullhorn and shouting orders at the Twin Towers.
- in 2003, when he parachuted onto the Yale campus, his "Mission Accomplished" banner and victory speech both targeted primarily an audience of one: his father. This young man who had avoided the war of his generation and frittered away his service in the National Guard suddenly re-appeared dressed as a Top Gun pilot and warrior like his father, triumphing, at least in his speech and dress, over his milksop father and his own military service inadequacies.
- in 2004, he again displayed insecurity when he refused to face the 9/11 Commission alone and needed to have Vice President Lip Surley accompany him and sit by his side, playing a role of a substitute father, advisor, comforter, libido enhancer and Darth Vader role model. Steroids have helped immensely in realizing these goals.
- in 2006, when his father was agitating behind the scenes to replace Field Marshall Rumpelstilskin, President Wondershrub responded to the removal pressure by asserting, against his father's influence, "I'm the Decider and I decide what's best." When asked about his father's influence, he proclaimed "I'm the Commander in Chief."

These behaviors reveal an unhappy mix of power and inadequacy. To hide these contradictory feelings, he early-on developed a number of psychological defenses. In his school years he played the role of a playboy, even becoming at times a clown. His long and heavy drinking allowed him to anesthetize feelings of inadequacy with feelings of levity, free spiritedness and debauchery.

Another defense has been recourse to writing his memoirs. We understand from unnamed high sources in the Red Cross that the president spends his days in captivity exactly as he did in the oval office in Washington: he sits hunched over a desk writing his memoirs, with undivided attention to his legacy. This exercise is frustrating for him as we understand he has yet to be able to put a word on paper without input from Vice President Surley.

The greatest psychological defense has been fundamentalist religion. He lets it be known to the world at large but, more importantly to himself, that his decisions are directed by God. As he puts it, it is "my gut" alone that makes his decisions, as he has often told reporters, thus equating his claim of unreflective spiritual inspiration to a set of infallible instincts inaccessible to others. His gut is God's mouthpiece. Indeed, God shares it with the Vice President. It is not only that Wondershrub is now infallible but that he <u>alone</u> is.

This identification of his own "gut" with God's will has great advantages in political therapy. It creates the perfect defense against doubt or uncertainty about the right decision. To follow his "gut" means to receive personal communication from God with an assurance of infallibility for whatever decisions he makes, including decisions in specialized fields like medicine or climatology. Any questioning of his gut strikes him as a rejection of his personal divine revelation about these and indeed all areas of human knowledge.

Being "born again" also allows him to see himself as having overcome all the inadequacies of his youth – his drinking, drugs, sex excesses, draft evasion, failed businesses, and poor academic records. Being born again allows him to be a new man, no longer incompetent but restored to a kind of divine omnipotence by reason of his fundamentalist partnership with the divine. The earthy father has indeed yielded to a Heavenly Father. When journalist Bob Woodward asked him if he'd consulted his human father before invading Iraq, he replied, "He is the wrong father to appeal to in terms of strength. There is a Higher Father that I appeal to."

One result of being born again, paradoxically, is that Wondershrub has become not only infallible but also a bully. His threat "You're either with us or against us" appears as a classic bully schoolyard slogan. His doctrine of pre-emptive strikes falls into the same bully attitude. He also uses mocking, sarcasm, teasing, name calling -- "Turd Blossom," "Mr Oscar Ozone"-- to insult and subjugate others. He is driven by the need to make others feel inferior to him. Labeling others with belittling names allows him to control them: He becomes their creator, they his creatures. He brings them into existence by naming them and defining their role, thereby marking them for an existence inferior to his.

His favorite game at Yale appears to have been one called "Global Domination," where he was well known for taking the most risks. In athletic events he would insist that points be played over again, usually claiming he wasn't ready. He would force opponents who had beaten him to replay him on his own terms and turf until he could beat them. He regularly interrupted fellow students studying in the university library by asking them to play games with him, thereby interfering with their studying for exams, a task he found irksome.

The psychic result appears as a blend of disdain for contemplation and an embrace for impulsive decision-making, with the emphasis on decisiveness rather than insight. Coupled with this is an effort to hide any inner feelings of compassion by transferring any lingering pain onto others. His remarkable drive for power to control and torture other human beings and his delight in Texas executions ("Oh, please don't kill me, please don't," as he mocked Ms. Tucker) show his true lack of compassion, notwithstanding the contrary slogan of his campaign.

The conflicts among these defenses generate unconscious dissociative states leading to confusion of loyalties, as appear in some of his more famous malapropisms:

• "They [the terrorists] never stop thinking of ways to harm our country and our people and neither do we"

• "There is no doubt in my mind that we should allow the world's worst leaders to hold America hostage, to threaten our peace, to threaten our friends and allies with the world's worst weapons."

Another useful defense appears as the excuse of not being required to account for his behavior. He dislikes questions in general. However, he especially dislikes questions that make him put into words his self-justifying gut instincts, his private revelation from above, if you will. As he told Bob Woodward, "I'm the commander – see, I don't need to explain – I do not need to explain why I say things….I don't feel like I owe anybody an explanation." Being commander in chief, being at war and operating as the nation's "Decider" reinforces this defense: his times are so urgent, his decisions so momentous that his judgment should never be questioned. He is not only the Decider; he is the Infallible One.

In the period after release of the Iraq Study Group Report, one can see how Wondershrub's defenses conflict with his drive for power and triumph over others. He felt the report showed his father vicariously dictating to him – after all, it had been co-authored by a person he knew as an ally and confident of his father. The report became the devil tempting him to return to failure once again. Instead, against the unanimous voices counseling to the contrary, he chose escalation in Iraq, the one course of action that kept alive in his mind the fiction that his personal success – victory in Iraq -- lay ahead in a reachable future.

The psychic strength of President Wondershrub The Lesser is this: If you act like you're confident and competent, then you are indeed. This is the power of positive thinking in a person whose assertiveness coexists with fear of failure and disdain for authority, beginning with his father and extending to the other two branches of government that, in his mind, deserve only to be ignored with the same hauteur he treats his father.

An organic basis appears for these psychological problems. Our analysis of a sample of his brain material, taken from him with the help of a psychic purgative in prison, reveals the densest element yet known to science: Shrubcronium, a solid mass held together by dark forces called morons and surrounded by minute particles called peons, working in subjection to a dominating substitute father figure, Vice President Lip Surley, to create a central fixation known as a "Critical Morass." President Wondershrub stands at the center of this morass like the conductor of a disharmonious orchestra, one who does not know how to read the score but wields the baton to make noise of his choosing. Whether it's music is irrelevant; noise is the goal, conducting the means.

Really Unruly: Wow, quite a report! I don't know if this wiretapping is such a good idea even if it did acquire this unflattering report. Perhaps we have Vice President Surley's wiretapping policies to thank for accessing this report. What's your own reaction, Dr Goopooh, (*pointing finger*) to this evaluation of our beloved President?

Dr Goopooh: Psychiatry is like the Bible: you can make it say whatever you want if the subject matter can be made to appear sufficiently divine.

11

Decision of the United States Supreme Court in the case of President Wondershrub and the United States of America vs. the Kingdom of Belgium and the International Court of Justice

Justice Antediluvian Scorpio, its author, reads aloud the Supreme Court's presidential abuse opinion at the Revolving Door Entrance to his Star Chambers.

SCORPIO, J.

The nature of this case concerns repeated torture of the basest sort against the President of a sovereign country , which incidentally is my own, [1] who has been held incommunicado without charges or chance to prove his innocence in any court of law, including in the captors' own courts, while being subjected to daily interrogations, whippings, beatings, being bitten repeatedly by German Shepherd dogs, forced to disrobe, appear with a naked hyena, and perform vile sex acts before the cameras of his foreign captors, and subjected to bodily purgations and psychiatric examinations now being leaked to the lowest levels of the general public! The legal question before this Court is whether this treatment violates our Eighth Amendment's "cruel and unusual" standard, indeed whether it violates the laws of any civilized country in the world. Can anyone believe that is a serious question?

---

[1]   The fact that he is the president of my own country and that he has again kindly invited me to join him on our annual quail hunting expedition in the lovely hinterlands of Texas plays no part in this decision, and deserves no mention here apart from my intention to accept his generous invitation again.

To answer that question requires that, for the first time in my distinguished career, I adopt a contextualist approach to the law as aptly expressed by my colleague Justice Higher. This approach requires a modification of my former constitutional approach, justified in this rare instance by the presidential subject who is the central issue in this torture case. The President's dire condition requires a more elastic theory of constitutional interpretation suitable for him alone. If we narrowly adopt only the meanings of the words "cruel and unusual" as these meanings existed at the time our country began, of course such vile torture would be acceptable now because it was acceptable then. But times change; once-free presidents become captive of a foreign power, a plight seemingly unforeseen by our Founding Fathers. Our colonial values evolve over time into moral values more sophisticated than existed at the birth of our nation. More exists in our Constitution than the explicit meanings of its dated words. Indeed, our Founders seemed to have had a future in mind for this country, or at least for Presidents as yet unborn or held captive when they first wrote three centuries ago

Our Founding Fathers realized full well that the rigid language of the First Amendment coexisted with colonial laws prohibiting libel, slander, obscenity, and inciting to riot. The juxtaposition of the Eighth Amendment with the First Amendment's prohibition of any law restricting free speech ("Congress shall make no law infringing the exercise of free speech...") shows that the Eighth Amendment cannot be read narrowly as a literal prohibition of <u>all</u> speech at the time of its adoption. Honoring such literalism today would invalidate the contrary laws of that time, including well established profanity, blasphemy, and libel prohibitions, not to mention prohibitions of public obscenity, exemplified by the indecent Manikin Pis of the President's captors, recalling the Psalmist's prayer, "*Renes nostras ad te, Domine, dirige,*" a clearly unacceptable literalism of "Direct our kidneys to you, O Lord."

In a more nuanced contextualist analysis, the cruel tortures inflicted, for example, by Chief Justice Jeffrey on the longsuffering Reverend Titus Oats, a man of the cloth and Founder of Quaker Oats, of necessity appear morally unacceptable today. We must accept the principle that morals evolve over time, just as oats come to take precedence over flour or as purgatives eliminate the old to make room for the new. No civilized country of the world with clocks, watchpieces, penultimate pendula or pendulous penumbrae or other legal pendants recording the movement of time could accept any conclusion about *rigor mortis* when our President's fate lies in the judicial balance [2]

In an evolving view of the legal values that define a maturing society, the extreme torture inflicted on our beloved President Wondershrub by these insensitive foreigners violates not only every principle of our evolving human rights slogans but also the moral principles of humanity everywhere! [3]

The laws of foreign countries confirm that not a single civilized country in the world would inflict such tortures on a fellow human being who is our President, Commander in Chief, and National Decider! Human rights are rights of the human being everywhere regardless of nationality or national boundaries! These laws confirm the rights existing at least implicitly in our own Constitution for all persons of all nations, whether residing here or in foreign nations like Old Europe. Scripture scholars know well Leviticus 19:34, which is legally controlling here: "The alien living with you must be treated as one of your native-born. Love him as yourself, for you were aliens in Egypt."

This view cannot plausibly be seen as merely one judge's opinion. In a private conversation with me this morning, my good friend, the Vice President in Charge of Waterboarding, reliably informed me that inherent executive privilege protects his office as well as that of the President from tortures acceptably inflicted on lesser citizens of our nation. Though this communication came to me orally rather than in

---

[2] As my older fellow countrymen liked to express it with reference to the passage of time, *Sic transit gloria mundi*, a principle of constitutional interpretation more flexible than the antiquated notion that all words of the Constitution retain today only the meanings existing at its drafting. *Verba movent, exempla trahunt.*

[3] As eloquently stated, for example, in the annual human rights reports disseminated by this administration's Departments of State and Justice, copies of which I have in my overflowing classics library and which I daily feel an urge to read Suffice it to say that these annual human rights reports set a high standard for recognizing human rights outside the borders of an individual sovereign state such as ours, particularly where that sovereign state has realized human rights under the well-established and nearly universal penultimate principle of parsimonious penumbra.

a legal document, I consider it an exalted utterance and award it the credence that befits the Vice President's inherent power to define the scope of his own inherent powers and the extent of his own executive powers.

We conclude -- or at least I do -- that Belgium's abominable torture of President Wondershrub remains anathema to the evolving principles of human decency. We order that it must stop. After all, it's not just a game! If the International Court of Justice or the Human Rights Court in Straussbourg or the InterAmerican Court lack the verbal power, then some Court somewhere – I have in mind this Court of mine –must assert itself to serve as a beacon for human dignity in these prisoner torture cases, at least regarding our beleaguered President.

For as our patriot Patrick Henry [4] himself intended to imply, though without saying so, these rights inhere in every human being apart from national boundaries, as we readily discover when that tortured person is my President.

Those on this court who disagree with this decision continue to be even greater idiots. The delusional is no longer marginal but extends even to my dissenting colleagues on this Court of mine, whom I salute with this time-honored Sicilian gesture (*his right hand gestures abruptly with a wrist flip outward from his chin*). [5]

---

[4]   This Court must take judicial notice of the substantial changes made in the recipe for the " Oh Henry" candy bar, as required by current FDA health standards more exacting than obtained in the colonial days of Patrick Henry when he began his revolutionary candy business with Paul Revere, another patriot, by the way, revered to this very day as the founder of Revereware – wares that, incidentally, I employ in my own kitchen while eating Quaker Oats every morning after my morning constitutional. *Necessitas non habet legem.*

[5]   The original meaning of this term appears in the ancient Hebrew "Raca," which meant then the same idiocy as it means today with regard to the dissenters on the Sanhedrin or on this Court or in a sovereign state such as ours, particularly where that sovereign state has realized human rights under the well-established and nearly universal penultimate principle of parsimonious penumbra.

PS My many admirers in this nation's legal community will note with disappointment that my eloquent opinion today appears unusually brief by comparison with my typically more effusive encyclicals, particularly compared to my earlier contrary opinion on this same subject of prisoner torture. Brevity offers some solace to my admirers. Shorter opinions such as this free up my lesser judicial colleagues to engage in the all -important task of scholarly reading of great literary works, medieval chants, Latin quotations, plays and poems so crucial for cultivating in the public eye an enhanced image of judicial wisdom, an erudition my lesser colleagues especially need to cultivate, one too easily lost in the mundane of trials, hearings and boring court decisions, excluding mine today, of course. Ancient wisdom, not modern decision-making, remains the hallmark of this Court and of the learning my erstwhile colleagues ought to aspire to but universally fall below.

This opinion's brevity in other part stems from a chance but memorable airport encounter with Sister Helen Prejean of *"Dead Man Walking"* who told me in a crowded waiting area exactly what she thought of my capital punishment jurisprudence. I cannot repeat in detail this nun's street level terminology here because it was not expressed in Latin or Italian, my mother tongues, nor does it reflect well on either church or state. Suffice it to say, however, that as a brief gesture of my good faith, I am today sending copies of my decision today – the part authored by me, of course, without the idiotic dissents – directly to her as well as to the House of Shrub, since President Wondershrub's location in his tragic captivity continues to be secret, illegally, I must add. I am also enclosing a personally autographed photo of me and my family, signed personally as "Luvi", my nickname for my intimates. *Amor vincit omnia.*

12

Tour of the Presidential Garden of Eden Theme Park

Secretary Heartfelt of the United States Department of Education and Reverend Geraldine Fallsoon lead a group of elders from the 5th Pentecostal Baptismal Evangelist Fundamentalist Church through the Presidential Garden of Eden Theme Park extending from the South Lawn of the White House to the Jefferson Memorial.

Secretary Heartfelt:

On behalf of the United States Department of Education, it's such a sacred privilege for me to show you elders around this Garden of Eden Theme Park, the newest addition to our national park system incorporating our "no child left behind" principles. We conduct this tour today, of course, with hearts heavily burdened by the continuing captivity of our beloved President whose vacant office looks out directly upon this park. Let us remember him in our thoughts and prayers as we walk humbly through the park he dreamed of creating for many years before his Belgian Captivity.

This theme park, of course, enshrines the many important archeological discoveries made during this administration's continuing Biblical excavations in the Middle East, the very birthplace of our nation. It also serves to underscore this administration's commitment to a mandatory faith-based education in which no child or dogma is left behind or unsuckled.

Reverend Fallsoon (*praying*): It has been just such a personal and sacred calling for me, O Father above, to answer Thy Calling to serve my mission on this administration's advisory board charged with mandating faith-based doctrines in the curricula of our public schools! I know I speak for the entire evangelical community, O Father above, in saying that we just see this theme park's proximity to the White House as a reflection of the close interplay, even identity, between church and state in this administration. We are just so thrilled, O Father, that the former wall separating church and state has been dismantled, like the Berlin Wall, as a vestige of the religious cold war, and now moved to the Mexican border to stop   illegal immigration. We thank Thee for answering our prayers beyond our expectations!

Secretary Heartfelt: A wonderful thought, indeed! Now back to our tour! Let's now take these people of God around to the celestial gates and then we'll visit the sacred exhibits. Here, around the pearly entrance gates , (*pointing upward*) you see that the park enjoys being well protected by high stone levees from any flooding from the rising glacier waters in   the Potomic River over there (*pointing*). Once our visitors pay their admission price here at the "Heavenly Gates" entry booth – admission fees are waived, by the way, for all war veterans in wheelchairs—park rangers transport them in these miniature chariots of fire directly to the visitors' center. The rangers driving the chariots dress not in National Park uniforms but as Old Testament figures – the most popular are Moses, Abraham and King David. Rangers may not choose costumes of Cain and Abel nor Pharaoh or Judas Iscariot.

The visitor center before you is an exact replica of Noah's Ark, but much bigger, of course. It is entirely made of wood from the True Cross. Its cabins serve as park offices. The lower decks contain stalls for ticket sellers and concession stands for Biblical souvenirs like, for example, neon replicas of Moses' Burning Bush or little statuettes of the Ten Commandments. There you can also find, of course, glacier drinking water fountains by all the rest rooms.

All children and parents can visit the Ark's kennels. These kennels hold pairs of the world's seven remaining animal types, hippos, rhinos, and other kinds I forget. The Bible, as you know, gives us dominion over them to do with as we wish. Their stalls take up about one tenth of the deck, less than Noah used for the more numerous pairs of animals living at the time of the Great Flood. This entire exhibit shows us the meaning of our dominion over animals, even extinct ones.

Let's continue down this pathway named, incidentally, the "Dead Sea Strolls" after those famous biblical manuscripts found when Moses liberated the Israelites by parting the Dead Sea. Over there (*pointing*) the park proudly displays a "Domestic Servant" Exhibit next to the entry gates. Leviticus in chapter 25 says that we may possess slaves, provided they are purchased from neighboring nations. Secretary Brunhilde has plans to travel to Canada and Mexico next week to negotiate a treaty permitting us to buy their citizens at a modest price and resell them here as slaves. Such a treaty may offer an opportunity to put some lower-class foreigners to work. At the main desk of this same exhibit park ministers handle paperwork for our nation's parents wishing, pursuant to Exodus 21:7, to sell their daughters directly into slavery, thus making it possible to bypass having to use our neighbors' citizens as our slaves. Our thanks and blessings, of course, go to these generous parents of teenagers, as well as to those who adopt this plan as a solution for our immigration problem.

From the top deck of the massive Ark visitors enjoy an overview of the entire park. By the way, we in the national park ministry like to call this park our "promised land," because we've wanted this park here on the South Lawn for such a long time. The offices near the gangplank over there (*pointing*) house the Prophetic Accounting Services, ("PAS"), where ordained accountants, well versed in the Book of Revelation, perform the Biblical math necessary to determine accurate numbers of those saved and damned. These numbers appear constantly updated on the flashing ticker-tape signs just above the entrance. To date, reading the current figures as of this hour, we know that 15,666 born-again Christians have been saved. They are all in our Bible Belt, mostly in Texas. They are all white and members of our churches. At present all other humans appear hopelessly damned. No one has yet been saved from any so-called "blue state" or from any other country of the world. Our biblical accountants are as busy as Mary and Martha to find their current addresses so they can send billing notices to the Elect informing them that they have been found worthy to be numbered among the happy few.

Next door is a casino where born-again Christians may buy lottery tickets to see if they can be made worthy to be numbered among the elect. You will note that the casino, however, has no gambling devices of any kind because God does not play dice with the world. We thank Thee, O Father above, (*praying*) that our prayers for our sacred Salvation Calculus have been answered so fully in these numbers, and we beseech Thee that they increase a hundred-fold, or at least enough to include us among your Elect!

As they disembark from the Ark, visitors receive a free blessing from our pastoral guides standing at the end of the gangplanks . There they also bestow on the children and parents of all religions a personal laying- on of hands, which is included in every admission ticket.

Let's walk along. this path through this grove of figs and olives.to the next exhibits. As we leave the visitor center, you will see that every building and exhibit here features a coin-operated drinking fountain with fresh glacier water, a true holy water piped in directly from our Glacier Memorial Park and from the formerly icy North and South Poles.

We are so honored to have with us today the very esteemed person responsible not only for blessing these glacier waters but also for caring for the President's spiritual wellbeing itself, right Reverend?

Reverend Fallsoon: Exactly right, Secretary Heartfelt. In fact, as you elders may not yet know, I have just today assumed the ministry of White House chaplain and confessor to the President, to begin as soon as our beloved President returns from his terrible Belgian Captivity, a rendition not unlike that of the Babylonian Captivity we read about in Exodus. (*praying*) O, Father, we beseech Thee that our President might merit a similar Exodus from Belgium!

My presidential calling is not only to act as chaplain but also as his confessor --- that is, to forgive any sins he might improbably commit, a ministry we know cannot be realized until his terrible captivity ends. We will be holding a prayer service for him in the Oval Office tonight, with a candlelight procession led by the National Park Service from the Department of Justice   right through this blessed theme park, down to the Jefferson Memorial, where the Department of the Inferior is also conducting a continuous   prayer vigil. (*praying*) O Father, that Thou might restore him to us in a Second Coming!

Here on the right bank, right by the Tree of Knowledge of Good and Evil transplanted from Iraq, you see the tombs of Adam and Eve recently discovered by our troops in Iraq. (*praying*) It is just so touching,

O Father, that they rest here side by side, despite their culinary differences, right here by the tombs of their children, Cain and Abel, the progenitors of the entire human race.

Just yesterday, in anticipation of the park's expansion, former Inspector General Ashpit personally conducted an anointing and vesting ritual for Adam family descendents to clothe their nakedness, anointing them with sacred oils found in the original Garden of Eden site in Iraq. On the top surface of Adam's tomb you see under glass this portion of Adam's Rib also discovered by our conquering troops during the recent Iraq crusade. The genital parts, of course, are fully clothed. On top of Eve's tomb sits this laminated photograph of her children, Cain and Abel, to whom she was very attached. Eve we revere to this very day as a devout Christian woman who, we are told, read her Bible daily.

Here, in this deep pit, lies the park's next exhibit – the "Serpent's Den." This den, personally designed by Vice President Lip Surley using his own mansion as a model, contains real life animations of the dastardly serpent who led our forefathers and foremothers, indeed all of us, into sin in the Garden by eating of the forbidden Apple. This large reptile cage contains a fierce model of the detested serpent. Indeed, this is where we store the cages needed to transport animals. The vile serpent himself is represented, as you see, by this stone sculpture, faithful to the text, showing Eve crushing the serpent's head who lies in wait for her heel. The serpent's face bears an exact likeness of Senator Hillarious!

This exhibit displays more than mere animation: we are proud to exhibit here a real life vulture representing Satan himself. Like Lucifer, the prince of devils, this enormous vulture is very proud, very bright, and, of course, a paradigm of evil. Though he seems very evil himself, as befits a devil -- look at his massive beak and monstrous claws -- he knows well the difference between good and evil. He confronts visitors by harassing and pecking at those who are morally good and caressing and embracing those who are evil, for these evil ones belong to him. His besotted nest sits on a limb at the top of the adjacent Tree of Knowledge of Good and Evil. We should give him a wide berth because he's likely to try to snatch a mouthful of our flesh as we walk by!

Secretary Heartfelt: Let's move on now to this next exhibit, the anointing and rapture hands-on memorial. Here National Park Ministers personally anoint visiting schoolchildren with blessed Hallibuttox sunblock oils to prepare them to take the "Rapture Ride" that catapults them high up into the heavens and parachutes them back to earth into the reflecting pools surrounding the Avenging Angel statue. Those who are unclean because of the abomination of homosexuality, however, are catapulted far into space to return from orbit only after they agree to have their abomination reversed, which can be accomplished in the Pussy Galore Transfiguration Spa, where any unnatural sexual orientation can be returned to its original proper design, to become, as Nature intended, a pearl of great price.

Near the Rapture Ride is the Rapture Ready Index, a control panel containing digital time clocks showing factors predicting the Coming of the Great Rapture, such as the crime rate, wild weather, heat, and, of course, "the mark of the beast," the number 666, as in 666 Pennsylvania Avenue. This is, unfortunately, as close as we can come in this world to pinpointing the expected arrival date of this Great Rapture described for us in the Book of Revelation. This joyous ride ought to give some idea of the thrill of that ultimate journey after the toils of this vale of tears.

Over here, next to the Rapture Ride, lies the sports field where seminary students may play soccer and other sports, but not football, of course, because Leviticus chapter 11 warns us that touching the skin of a dead pig makes one unclean. Remember, however, as President Wondershrub assured us before his painful captivity, that a man and a pig can co-exist. Scorpio Scholars are hard at work reconciling these texts on the basis of questions submitted in the park's Question and Answer Box over there (*pointing*). Why, just yesterday these scholars began addressing this question submitted by Reverend Allen: "If whosoever shall not fall by the sword or by famine will then fall by pestilence, why should the devout bother bathing?"

Across the street stands an exhibit we affectionately call the "Hell Hole." It's an exhibit primarily created for the benefit and edification of young children. Parents can bring their children here to peer through these downward-facing periscopes to see condemned persons below screaming as they are consumed in flames for sins like homosexuality, liberalism and touching pigskin. These sins are the stuff screams are made of. If you look down the scopes carefully to the bottom of the pit you'll see well-known atheists like Nietzsche, Sartre, Hitler and Mr. Sodom and Ms. Gomorrah writhing in pain in the flames. A scarlet devil prances about in the center of the flames screeching to visiting schoolchildren that, unless they abandon their sinfulness, they too will burn forevermore in these eternal flames. Our goal in the Hell Hole, of course, is to maximize this uplifting message of eternal immolation.

Reverend Fallsoon recommends that the ideal age for children to visit the Hell Hole is just before kindergarden , though children younger than five enjoy free admission. Children suffering nightmares receive a free second visit where these play-actor devils hold them tightly on their fiery laps! That ought to leave a warm impression indeed! No child is left behind here!

Another exhibit of special interest to our young visitors is the "Respect for Life" exhibition. Actually several exhibits are included here. One shows the President's private collection of stem cells, each male in its own Petri dish and females in a Pauline dish. Each has a name and a Republican registration card already! Down the hallway, lining these long walls (*pointing*), this exhibit displays millions of small pictures of aborted fetuses, all resulting from the tragic *Roe v Wade* decision. Then, across the same hallway, on the side we call the "Death Row Gallery," we have an exhibit of pictures of all the nearly six thousand human criminals put to death, properly, since our country's founding. A noose serves as the frame of each condemned person's picture. The walls above these pictures display scriptural quotations authorizing capital punishment, as, for example, Exodus 35:2 requiring the death sentence for anyone found working on the Sabbath.

In the central nave of this chamber sits a real electric chair where visiting children can enjoy a unique "hands-on" experience. As they are strapped into this chair, they feel a mild jolt of electricity, as a shocking reminder to them of how our faith requires us to dispatch those who violate our fundamental values. The small booth in the corner of this exhibit houses Scorpio Legal Fellows whose scholarship, we expect, will eventually resolve any inconsistencies in this exhibition hall.

Next, as we move along the Dead Sea Strolls, here at the center of the park we find the "Jonah the Whale" exhibit. It's really a big whale constructed of plaster and neon lights sitting atop a wooden hull also made from wood from the True Cross. See his big mouth and how wide it opens when I press this "on" button! (*demonstrating*) Look inside at his big teeth and the gullet extending like a mushy tunnel right into his big belly! When he gets anything in his mouth, he chews it up! When he moves his teeth, his neon eyebrows arch, he breaks into a smile, and the audio plays "When the Saints Go Marching in."

Jonah of the Old Testament, you know, lived for three days in the belly of a whale just like this, but of course that was well before the advent of the modern shredding machinery now housed inside him. Jonah's belly stretching before you is large enough to hold any number of human prey today, so be careful as you approach him.

Jonah also serves as the the park's debris collection system . When we dump picnic debris here or trash or, say, the bodies of dead or dying animals who fall over the Falls there (*pointing*) in front of his mouth, he sucks them right in, chews them up, digests and compacts them and then spits them out his tail end! Here, in front of Jonah, are the Great Falls, where this huge waterfall connects the Potomac River to the waters churning about right before Jonah's mouth. The inscription over the Falls comes from the Prophet Amos: "Justice Shall Roll Down Like the Waters."

The park's many streams and canals flow right over the Falls here and then down Jacob's ladder directly into the pool before Jonah's mouth, and then inside his gullet, where the floating debris collects, gets "ingested," and then "digested" in the large shredders and compacters in Jonah's belly that crush the debris into compost and oil. The precious oil residue is diverted in his belly to flow into the glass oil pipelines you see here (*demonstrating*). Each year on Groundhog Day we re-enact the biblical story of the swine being turned loose, hurtling over the cliff like lemmings and being swept over the Falls directly into Jonah's gaping mouth. Jonah's glass exterior, of course, makes everything inside visible to spectators on the outside, so these spectators can see the dismembering of each of these swine just by peering through Jonah's glass- enclosed stomach. President Wondershrub used to say proudly, when he was with us in the flesh, that his was an open pipeline administration!

After Jonah's internal grinding is complete, the compost residue exits the tail end of Jonah for distribution around the many Middle Eastern plants, palms and fig trees in the park as well as at the monuments of the adjoining Jefferson Memorial. If you dare to throw your hot dogs or hamburgers into Jonah's big mouth, you get some small idea how the debris shredding and oil squeezing operations actually work! Just kidding, of course. These dials and guages next to Jonah's tail register the components of the compost – how much fat, how much waste, how much bone, and, of course, how much oil the machinery is generating. That's the meaning of a market-based economy!

Reverend Fallsoon: Here's the next exhibit, the Fossil Science Museum, demonstrating that religion and science suffer no conflicts, science as properly understood, of course. On this plaque at the entrance you find quotes from the famous Tennessee monkey trial that disproved evolution. In the labs down this hallway (*demonstrating*), Bobby Jones University Turd Blossom Fellows are working with "text-tubes" to distinguish, via scripture references, the 4% of genes distinguishing humans from chimps. Over there you see the Ancient Fossils Exhibit explaining how these fossils appear to secular scientists to be millions of years old when, in actuality, we know they can be no older than six thousand years at most. We now know, thanks to this research, that the Great Flood washed these fossils to these locations and prematurely aged them, making them look older than they really are . The devoted work of our Turd Fellows, as approved by President Wondershrub himself, has also revealed that some heathen scientists go about the world carefully imbedding these fossils in the world's rocks with an aging agent, as a way of challenging our faith in the true youth of the earth.

Over in the next building is the Inerrancy Exhibition Hall where specially trained scriptural exegetes show how the world was created in 24/7 and how light was created before the sun. Scorpio Fellows – Biblical scholars chosen for research grants from the Justice's Originalism Foundation – reconcile the two creation stories in Genesis and the differing Nativity stories in Matthew and Luke. They are also reconciling the differences between the choirs of Cherubim and

Seraphim. There was once some difference between them, but these differences have now been happily resolved!

Over in that corner of the park you see an anatomy laboratory where our born-again medical scholars seek the purposes for such human anatomical features as the appendix, tonsils, and male nipples. Specially trained medical personnel work in the adjoining laboratory to re-configure the human appendix as a surrogate bladder and to transform male breasts into protrusions as fulsome and nurturing as Eve enjoyed before being deflated by the Fall. Any Bible-damaged visitors impaired by a symbolic reading of The Word can be restored to Biblical health here by undergoing therapy in our Lab of Inerrancy.

Secretary Heartfelt: Next, on your left, the exhibit with the massive gyrating iron tongue is the Tower of Babel, commemorating the development of evangelical language from the time of Adam down to present–day political uses. Mr Justice Antediluvian Scorpio himself serves as a volunteer guide here on weekends. He often conducts seminars on prophecy. On special occasions he presents demonstrations on "speaking in tongues," an Old Testament skill he finds indispensable for eloquent judicial opinion writing. He is also much sought-after in exegetical circles for his knowledge of the root meanings of words. He is compiling, even as we speak, an "originalism dictionary" containing only the root meanings of all our words.

Eloquent speakers, homilists and political leaders will be buried right here (*pointing*) in the Babbling Brook Cemetery at the base of the Babel Tower as a reminder of the creative political uses of The Word. This left side of the Babel Tower will permanently house a copy of our President's honorary D. Litt. degree, so improperly taken from him. The President himself has expressed a fond desire to be buried here as well and to have his tongue encased in sterling silver, as was done, as you know, for the sacred tongue of former President Dioxin, who so sadly has gone before us in faith.

Here, by the waters of Shiloh, you find the park's souvenir stand, where visitors may buy postcards of the Garden, plus autographed pictures of Adam and Eve. Today we have a discount on Bible Belts made of leather from extinct polar bears formerly living in the Alaskan Wildlife Preserve and at the North and South Poles. We also sell holy cards with pictures of our famous religious forebears like the apostles,

Moses, his Burning Bush, plus pictures, busts and books of modern day prophets like, for example, the Reverend Robert Patrickson, one of our trustees, pictured here lifting one of his thousand pound weights. The Burning Bush picture reminds me, by the way, to mention the Middle Eastern spa over there to your left (*pointing*) where an exact replica of Moses' Burning Bush heats the spa, the adjoining sauna featuring alabaster spices, and serves as a gathering place for Sunday bar-b-ques of infidels.

The street vendors here sell chocolate crucifixes that bleed red jam; we call them "Sweet Jesus Treats" as a reminder of His sweet passion. Young children love them! Here, too, you can buy photos of such Biblical Greats as, for example, Esau and Jacob, the one hairy, the other as smooth of head as Vice President Surley. Opps, he wouldn't laugh at that now, would he!

Reverend Fallsoon: As we head toward the exit, you see the two white trailers imported from Iraq serving as the park's official concession stands. Here park visitors can buy not only traditional American hot dogs, hamburgers and shakes but also the park's culinary specialties -- original scriptural food, like olives, figs, figburgers , figfries, freedom figs, locusts, locust poppers, locust fries, honey, of course, and milk and honey malts, these last served in cups containing the presidential seal. We just thank Thee, O Father, (*praying*) for providing this spiritual food to nourish our souls!

Secretary Heartfelt: Here's a concession stand called "Adam's Ribs" and another named "Eve's Eggs" – guess what you can get here! You can flavor today's special -- loaves and fishes -- with Lot's Pillars of Salt on the tables! This main concession stand also offers discounts on Reverend Rover's entire line of liberal purgatives. Today, you'll note, there's a one-day special on his "Bolus Bile Blaster" specially discounted for "blue state" visitors. The park's "Adam" and "Eve" restrooms stand conveniently nearby. Wedding ceremonies occur in the adjacent Song of Songs wedding chapel!

This concession also contains on the back wall a gilded portion of the original Apple – not, mind you, a replica, but the real Apple -- found in the Garden by our troops at the Tigres and Euphrates Rivers in Iraq during our continuing Hunnert Day crusade there. We have to hope that the Charwoman who operates this concession stand for the Joint Chefs of Staff never confuses that real Apple with any of the other delicacies she prepares here! She also can mix up a pretty strong testosterone cocktail, like the Vice President orders when he visits here along with the President, who, again, so needs our prayers in his modern-day Babylonian Captivity.

Reverend Fallsoon: Now, as we prepare to leave the park, you should know that park visitors can satisfy our country's mandatory continuing evangelical education right here. The national AIMS test will be given here in this cathedral before us that also serves as the park's bible college and graduation auditorium. Pastoral park rangers grade public school science exams right here on the premises! Students who pass this test receive whatever degree they need, from a grade school diploma or GED right on up to a Doctor of Divinity degree! No child is left behind!

Visiting this park is thus an easy way to satisfy each American's continuing biblical education requirement. Guests of all faiths can enjoy the picnic grounds adjoining the Tree of Knowledge of Good and Evil, just next to the Falls, to sit under the blessed shade of the Knowledge Tree to meditate upon The Word as they enjoy another culinary specialty, locust and honey shakes with loaves and fishes from the Dead Sea itself!

Finally, here at the park's exit, all departing visitors, regardless of creedal differences, receive personal anointing and blessings from our pastoral park rangers. The visitors' blessings don't stop there! Exiting visitors from all countries and religions receive a special treat: our Ranger Ministers immerse them three times in this baptismal font adjacent to Jonah's reflecting pools After this baptism the Rangers stamp their foreheads "saved" with this permanent red dye as they pass through the turnstiles, thereby assuring their eternal salvation. Our Sacred Accounting Office then records their names among The Elect. They're then given a bleeding "Sweet Jesus" jelly crucifex as a memento of their holy visit here.

Once the park is formally dedicated, we hope to see you all back here on your next visit to the White House! It's included in your White House tour ticket!

13
Press Conference in the White House Leaking Room

The Press Conference takes place in the crowded Circumlocution Vestibule to the White House Leaking Room. Secretary of State Brunhilde and Press Secretary Whiteout, along with his assistant Soothing Platter, preside. Platter plays a CD of "Pathetique."

Secretary Whiteout:

I am deeply saddened to report to you that today, at 1430 hours, military time, tourists in the Grande Place in Brussels, Belgium, found the body of President Wondershrub floating naked in the water pool circulating at the base of the statue of the unclothed Manikin Pis. This discovery occurred shortly after the Belgian Supreme Court announced it would not recognize the recent Justice Scorpio decision of our Supreme Court nor the parallel decision of the International Court of Justice prohibiting the inhumane treatment of an impaired presidential prisoner.

When tourists found him, the President's body was lacking the loincloth we understand he was forced to wear in his captivity. His torso appeared to be badly bruised. Dog bite marks and whipping stripes were abundant. His hands were tied behind his back. The Manikin Pis he had once bravely sought to clothe continued to function even as his body floated in its foul waters. The President's upper body was clad only in the remnants of a tattered Yale English Department T-shirt, the one previously worn by the same indecent Manikin.

The President was rushed to the 24 hour Urgent Care facility in the American Embassy down the street from the Grande Place. There, after a wait of several hours to verify his health savings plan , our dedicated American Embassy medical staff managed to work the

President in among scheduled patients. The doctor's first concern was to repair the President's most pressing medical condition, which was diagnosed as Stubborn Iraqtile Dysfunction Syndrome, or SIDS.

The medical staff tried heroically to remedy that malady but unfortunately found it too advanced for treatment. They gave the President an intimate neck massage, the kind he so often administered to foreign leaders, followed by a powerful Rasputin purgative. They then attended to his widespread stripes, malnutrition, and loss of blood from bone-deep dog bites, whippings and beatings. Despite the best efforts of our embassy's dedicated medical staff, President Wondershrub was reportedly pronounced dead at 1630 hours, military time, this afternoon.

Platter changes music to Mozart's "Requiem."

Whiteout (*wiping away tear*): I'll take a few questions. Little Sir Echo.

Q: Little Sir Echo, FAUX NEWS (*sobbing*): Why do you say "reportedly"? Is that a word of art or a word of fact for our press conferences? If our beloved President is in fact dead, how could this happen to a man so admired all over the world, especially in our studios? Will his torturers be caught and be brought to justice so we can do a crime show about it? Will we still be able to keep our TV studios in His Majesty's bedroom? Is his death for real or just "reportedly"?

A:Secretary Whiteout: Our information about the President's death comes from unnamed high government sources in this very administration. These unnamed sources tell us that they hope that these evil Belgian captors and violators of human rights will be brought to justice. Senior government officials in the White House Press Office will give you, Sir Echo, exclusive rights to any crime stories about his tragic death, if it occurred, or, for that matter, any other deadly crime stories you can generate about his criminal mistreatment. Fear is an important part of your work, as it is for ours as well. Your bedroom privileges will remain as long as this administration is in office, provided you do not disturb the President's picture books.

As to the "reportedly" part of your question, this office can only confirm matters expressly confirmed by the President himself. We are awaiting a signing statement from him to permit us to confirm his death, if it occurred or if it didn't.

Q:Bear Blitzkrieg, CANNED NEWS: What about the President's daily schedule? His appointments? Will there have to be some changes there? If he is dead, does he remain our Decider?

A:Whiteout: Changes to his schedule can only come from the President. He certainly still remains The Decider. He will have to let us know if he decides to make any changes in his scheduled activities. As you should know, changes to his daily schedule, like his workout routine, his reading of the funnies, his coloring and painting chores, his birth or even his death, remain as personal decisions for him alone to make under his inherent powers as Decider in Chief, without the need for explanation to anyone, even citizens such as you. Only a unitary President has the power to decide those sensitive matters, including whether to disclose such facts as his own death to the citizens of his own country.

Q: Peter Paula, Usable News: Well, how can he do that if he is dead, Whiteout? Or are you suggesting he is perhaps not dead? Or not fully dead yet? Or that his death is a diversion from your "unnamed government sources" to distract our nation's "criticizers" ? Or another secret kept from the American people?

A Whiteout: These are all good questions unless, of course, we decide they are bad questions. We have no further comment beyond what has previously been told you. This administration is opposed to leaks of all kinds, especially leaks involving the President's health conditions and above all, of course, facts about whether he is alive or dead, which are, of course, the most personal of all human affairs. Both the President and the Vice President are very private about their health , their conversations, their lives, their bodies, their steroids and especially their government decisions. Intruding on any of these would violate the basic American right to privacy, a paramount value of this administration that explains why only "unnamed sources" can speak for them on such personal matters.

This policy serves the good of the American people who cannot handle distracting news in the midst of their busy schedules. Any news about our much-loved President's passing, if it occurred, would be traumatic . If we have any further comments, we will alert you of our denials at that time or, if necessary, we won't.

Q Little Sir Echo, FAUX NEWS *(sobbing)*: How can it be that our only Lord President, if he is indeed dead, has been reaped so grimly by the Grim Reaper, well before his time?

A Whiteout: You may recall that a similar fate befell his mentor, Trick E. Dioxin, who also was reaped before his reaping was due. If President Wondershrub is indeed dead, anonymous official sources will arrange for his tongue to lie in state near the Tower of Babel in the Biblical Theme Park, just as was the case for the funeral of the sacred tongue of former President Dioxin.

Q Little Sir Echo, FAUX NEWS: When will the funeral, if there is one, occur? Can we have front row seats? What sad songs will be sung? Can we sing along too, if we promise to stay in tune?

A Whiteout: Just as soon as President Wondershrub informs unnamed high government officials that he is in fact dead and then allows official sources, on condition of anonymity, to confirm the basic fact of his death, and decides on the dimensions of his casket, you can rest assured of being right in the casket with him, songbook and all, provided you sing in harmony with his music. I don't see a problem there for you.

Secretary Brunhilde: We, of course, are profoundly upset at Belgian's ignoring of our American Supreme Court decisions, as well as its violations of international laws, its own laws, the Geneva Convention, the basic human rights cherished by all civilized peoples around the globe, as well as its explicit disdain for the decision of our own Justice Scorpio prohibiting torture of our beloved President. We are, of course, also very shocked at this indifference to democracy, freedom, the rights of man, universal brotherhood, the desires of peace-loving peoples everywhere, the respect due motherhood, fatherhood and applepiehood , as well as inner city flight, our beloved homeland hearths, the privilege of all major sexes to breast-feed in public with a flavor of their choice, and, of course, the American Peoples' unfettered right of unobstructed access to Patrick Henry's original candy bar recipe.

Later today, after signing a new Slave Exchange Treaty with Canada and Mexico, I will file a complaint under the Geneva Convention with the International Court of Human Rights as well as with the United Nations and the International Court of Justice in The Hague. We have no better friend than the International Court of Justice in The Hague. We consider any nation's ignoring the Geneva and Vienna Conventions to be the most egregious and unquaint violations of the most fundamental human rights, worldwide democracy, the rights of peace-loving peoples everywhere, the cause of undying freedom, the ideals of peace, justice and the American highways, our cherished vanilla ice cream with cherry pie, the right of every fan to sing "Take Me out to the Ballgame" at the seventh inning stretch, plus every citizen's innate right to worship assault weapons, sunbathe on the nation's North and South Pole beaches, and enjoy their God-given right to eat Quaker Oats of a flavor of their choosing, just as their individual consciences and our Constitution allow.

Q Little Sir Echo, FAUX NEWS: Will we be able to view the president's royal tongue lying in state? May we plant a flag in it? May we serve as official bearers of pall as pallbearers, carry the flag and put our FAUX logo on the casket?

A Whiteout: I can certainly guarantee you that you and indeed all patriotic Americans will be allowed to pay your respects to the President's tongue at the funeral, unless of course we decide you cannot. I can absolutely assure you that you will have an honored place as a pallbearer, though of course I can't promise that.

14

Eulogy by the Rev. Robert Patrickson at the bier of President Wondershrub

Reverend Robert Patrickson delivers the funeral eulogy for President Wondershrub at the Tower of Babel Exhibit of the White House Garden of Eden Biblical Theme Park. The Supreme Court Barbershop Dirge Quartet, conducted by Mr. Justice Scorpio in his black robe, with Mr. Justice Scorpolini as soloist, leads the congregation in singing "John Brown's Body." Former Inspector General Johnny Ashpit sprinkles blessed Hallibuttox Oils on the President's tongue, lying in state on a silver platter, under glass, next to his body.

Reverend Patrickson:

Dearly Beloved, our letter today, on this day of such lamentation, is taken from the last part of our old alphabet. It is the letter W, one of the humblest of all our letters.

What does this lowly W stand for? War? Wonder? Woe?

In the Third Revised New World Version at 1536, the large Book of Noah containing all our words defines "wonder" -- which begins with the very same W -- as having as its first meaning "the person, thing or event that causes astonishment." When Noah Webster wrote this entry on his Ark's deck during the 40 days of the Great Flood, he was inspired to give us yet another meaning of "wonder," a competing meaning that he describes as "the feeling of surprise, admiration and awe aroused by something strange."

Noah then gives us an exegesis of wonder. "Exegesis," my dear friends -- a technical word perhaps foreign to your ears -- is a Biblical scholar's spelling-bee term, meaning the scholarly search for the original or root meaning of a word. For example, our own Supreme Court Justice Antediluvian Scorpio, who is leading our dirge quartet at this very funeral, has himself written that the first or "root" meaning of a word constitutes its only meaning, such as the word "gay" having today the identical original meaning as in the ancient Christmas carol "happy and gay."

So what, then, my friends, appears as the true exegesis of this word "wonder"? Why, it seems to be none other than the ancient term "wundrian," which Noah himself tells us originally meant in the world's first days "to have curiosity sometimes mingled with doubt." For "wundrian" Noah gives us the example of "a person who wondered what happened." "To have curiosity sometimes mingled with doubt." To "wonder what happened." These are our linguistic guides for this difficult exegesis on this day of such lamentation.

Heads bowed and eyes closed, let us struggle together to interpret these troubling texts. Let us reflect on who, what or that which has brought forth in us this "feeling of astonishment, surprise and awe" about "something strange" causing us to "doubt" and "wonder" about "what happened?" Which of Noah's meanings from these ancient "W" texts helps explain this "Wonder" lying so disfigured before us?

Last week I was sunbathing on the top deck of my first class cruise ship sailing to my new Surf and Swim Center of Homeless Ministry being built on a resort island two miles from the North Pole. A cabin boy on this great luxury ship approached me and said, "Isn't the view wonderful?" Rising and girding my loins I responded unto him, "Amen, amen, I say unto thee, young man, heaven and earth have not revealed this view unto thee, but rather thy own eyeballs! Verily, thou are blest of all flesh, for thou canst find wonder in the warm sights and sounds around thee rather than seeking it in cool places far off! "

So surprised was this cabin boy, then, with wonder, and so are we, my friends, and so indeed are ye! The wonder is near, not far off at the North or even at the South Poles' balmy beaches. It is right before thine eyes, in this sacred tongue lying so eloquently here under glass.

But what is the meaning of "right before thine eyes?" In the Old Testament we read of Esau and Jacob , the sons of Abraham. "Esau is a hairy man, but I am a smooth man," Jacob tells us. How does the "hairy-ness" of Esau, if we can call it that without offending him, how does this "hairy-ness" relate to the smoothness of Jacob, like the smoothness of someone whose bald head glistens with emoluments of sacred oil, like our beloved Vice President Surley grimacing so hairlessly here before us?

Why, my friends, the true answer, of course, could not be clearer. Esau stands for the first meaning of wonder and Jacob represents the second meaning. Together these two Hebrew brothers show that the fullest interpretation of "wonder" lies not in these first or second meanings but only in the third meaning, in the ancient word "wundrian," originally connoting , as ye now know, to "wander amidst wonders causing us to question and doubt what happened right before our eyes in our very own day." Wonder , then, in <u>that</u> special sense, not in the Psalmist's sense of "Wonderful, Counselor, the Mighty King, the Everlasting Lord, the Prince of Peace."

The name "Wondershrub" certainly evokes childlike wonderment. A small child usually grows in age, wisdom and grace into adulthood by leaving behind the toys of childhood. For what is a child if not an adult? The Apostle Paul himself refers to this transitus to maturity by proclaiming "When I was a child, I played with the things of a child, but now that I am become a man I play with the things of a man." For what is an adult if not a child? Our prophet Wordsworth himself tells us that "the child is father of the man." And Augustine himself says "Tantillus puer et tantus peccator" – such a little child but such a big sinner, a wonder to behold. Yes, my friends, he who becomes a mature adult <u>leaves behind</u> the playthings of a child, the toy tanks, the comics, the airplanes, the educational awards, the toy soldiers, the manikins of one's youth. Yea, verily, he <u>leaves them behind</u>! Or, to take another scriptural example, behold the trees of the fields. For what is a tree if not a mature shrub? And what is a shrub if not a tree that is stunted? Has this kind of growth come to pass in the Wonder so Raptured to glory before our very eyes?

A devout woman operating a preschool nursery near my new soup kitchen at the South Pole exclaimed to me just last week "Let the Little Children Come unto Me." So it also appears with this Wonder who has made his own Second Coming unto us, to come before us on this cold slab, to lie here at our feet like a limp albatross, swaddled in these gilded lilies, reaped by the Grim Reaper before his time while playing with the toys of his youth. A Wonderchild, he was, or said he was, who sat on a throne with a claim of divine right. He thought of himself as one who, like Moses of old, came down from the high mountain to deliver a sacred message to his Chosen People, if only those Chosen knew how to listen. A divine Wonder disguised in human dress, some might say, or perhaps as a shrub-like tree? Or perhaps as a Prodigal Son? Or could it be, as the prophet expresses it, a lamb sadly led to the slaughter we know as SIDS? But as the Hebrew psalmist cautions us, "Not as the world thinks do I think."

In the days of old, just as in the days of the Great Rupture to come, those Chosen of the Lord will remove the beams from their own eyes in order to remove the mites from the eyes of others. Today we see before us this silver tongue lying so dumbly behind a veil, as under a glass darkly, as though passing through the narrow eye of a needle into a whitened sepulcher under a camel's loathsome nose spouting fire and brimstone. Those are our clear scriptural signposts showing us how to understand this wondrous tongue. Was it tongues of fire? Or speaking in tongues? By his stripes are we healed, or by the Word of his tongue alone? In the end, perhaps we are left only to wonder about wonder, just as Noah and his wife Joan of Ark were behooved to wonder when the torrential rains swept away their great collection of words in the raging waters of that Great Flood that, like Justice itself, rolls down the ages from Mount Ararat down to our very own time, yea, even unto our own Great Flood, Katrina.

My friends, what doth be the difficult lessons to be learned today from this awesome Wonder? Why, certainly one of the first is to give alms to the poor. This very day we have that opportunity to lighten the burden of the President's tortured passing, by relieving the medical burden borne by the entire grieving House of Shrub. We can give the saddened Shrubs alms this very day. The emergency medical services provided for President Wondershrub by the dedicated medical staff of our Embassy in Belgium exhausted his health savings plan. Today's collection is being taken to defray the medical expenses for which his health savings plan fell short. Please be generous as the House of Shrub, too, cannot afford to pay these medical bills and may have to convert to Christian Science.

Let us, then, cometh prostrate before this high altar of Babel, humbled by the impoverishment of President Wondershrub lying so disfigured here, and before the Vice President grimacing in pain before us, so sadly unable to embrace his fellow humans in this time of such great loss. Let us, united as one people, ponder the Wonder before us by joining hearts and voices to recite together the poor Shepherd's Psalm:

(*All recite*)

Wondershrub was our shepherd, we dwelleth in want
He anointeth our heads with Hallibuttox oil
He maketh trees to fall in national parks
He leadeth snowmobiles into the stillness of national forests
He restoreth our Apple and our Garden of Eden.

Every head bowed, then. All eyes shut. Lips closed. Voices stilled, one and all. Let us join our hands, one and all -- but not, please, those of the Vice President-- as we lament this Wonder named after a mere shrub not unlike Moses' Burning Bush, consumed in its own ashes, like unto Abraham willing to sacrifice his own nation's beloved sons, a prodigious Wonderchild who came unto us just as the scripture says, to bring us not peace but a sword.

My friends , what would ye do if ye found someone ye trusted taking a jackhammer to the foundations of thy home? For many years now the enemies of our nation's values have been pounding away with jackhammers at the foundations of thy homeland, claiming to construct their projects and platforms in the name of " trust me," in the name of that Great Power before whose name even the angels tremble. Could this Wonder have procured such jackhammers, perhaps even on the open market? Could he have jackhammered even at thy own foundations?

Recall the story of Jesus and the man possessed by devils. Jesus asked him, "How many are you?" "Legion" was their answer. Jesus then said to these devils, " I give you permission to enter those swine." The legion of demons then left the man we know as the Galarene demoniac and entered a herd of swine grazing nearby. When the demons entered them, the swine rushed to their deaths by being swept like lemmings into the surging waters of the nearby lake, over a Falls, and drowning (Mt 5-1-13).

How could this possibly happen to the friends of the Galarene demonic? To be swept up in surging waters like vile swine! To be consumed in raging waters like evil serpents! The prophet Isaiah himself spake in advance of the "hubris" or pride of these Babylonian demoniacs and their vile lemmings. Here are the prophet's exact words to us about pride:

> You said in your heart, I will ascend to heaven, I will raise my throne above the Stars of God. I will sit enthroned on the mount of assembly, on the utmost heights of the sacred mountain. I will ascend above the tops of the clouds. I will make Myself like the Most High" Isaiah, 14: 12-14.

Now, my friends, as well as you bearers of pall at this funeral, ye whom I know and especially ye dearly beloved whom I do not yet know, our Anglo-Saxon word "devil" comes from the Greek word *diabolos*, meaning "lying accuser" and from the old Aramaic word *abbadon*, which means the "destroyer." These ancient words, when taken in their original meanings, describe the devilish lies of the Prince of the Power of Darkness, the proud winged demon known as the "Great Vulture" or "Great Satan," and the evil legions he assembles around him in his cabins of power and powdered cabinets and powder rooms. These are the bad angels known collectively as the "Great Dragon" in the 12th book of Revelation, serving under the command of this loathsome Great Vulture, who took his bad angels to a watery death with him. (Ish. 7-9). This Devil Vulture is "a liar and the father of all lies" in John 8: 44. The Scriptures say of this Satan "He was murderous from the beginning, not holding to the truth, for there is no truth in him, the father of all lies" (John 8: 44). So I ask ye, once again: Could ye recognize this Great Vulture if he were to descend from the skies upon ye this very day?

What, then, shall we accept as our own personal calling on this day of such overwhelming wonder? Besides giving alms as just mentioned, our mission as bearers of pall behooves us to "drive out demons." (Mt 10, 7-8). As we persevere in this ministry of purgation and expulsion, we must see ourselves as others do, a Chosen People gathered solemnly here at this lofty Tower of Babel joined to the Oval Office by the thin drywall separating church and state . But something there is, as the prophet Frost tells us, something there is, my friends, that doth not love a wall. The Bible tells us to separate wheat from chaff, truth from falsehood, trust from deception, shrubs from mature trees, sons from fathers, but not church from state. We are reminded of that, you undoubtedly recall, at every wedding with the scriptural admonition "Let no man cast them asunder."

What, then, are these additional wonders right before thine eyes? Listen to this:

> "I say unto you, Anyone who says to his brethren 'Raca' is answerable to the Sanhedrin. And I say to you, Whoever says to his brethren 'you Idiot,' will be in danger of the fire of hell." (Matt 5, 21-23).

What is this strange word "Raca"? My friends, especially my friends who seek, with the Prophet Amos, to witness "justice rolling down like waters," the term "Raca" is an Aramaic word for contempt. It means to judge another person as an idiot or fool, like trash to be discarded or ignored. It is a term no follower of the Lord would use to describe his companions, not even in jest, certainly not in court. The people who misuse such a name for their own selfish gain fall under divine wrath: "You shall not misuse the Name" warns the Lord. (Ex. 20:7).

As I review the historical parade of civilization's power brokers, I find that the worldly emperors of wonder always have appropriated unto themselves power, pride, shock and awe. All history is replete with these figures. Look, my dear friends, look at Alexander the Great, who begat the sneering Attila the Hun; who begat the haughty Goths and Visigoths with their noisy battle cries and warring clubs; who in turn begat the annoying Moths and their habits of concealment; who in turn begat the Sloths with their private secrets; who begat Genghis Kahn and the Mongols with their foul breath; who in turn begat the warring Mohicans with their hairless Mohawks; who begat, in due time, the bellicose Tartars with their decaying teeth; who begat, in our own day, Sodom and Gomorrah and their unsmiling Sodomites; who begat, in the fullness of time, the Dean of the Darth Vader School of Ventriloquism, our beloved Vice President Surley, grimacing so painfully here today as he prepares to mount his throne of glory.

The prophet Samuel refers to a divisive day like this: "One spring day," he says, "when kings go off to war."(2 Samuel 11:1) What does it behoove us to understand of this bellicose prediction? The answer lies right before us, right at our lowly feet. Behold the lilies of the field: they toil not, neither do they spin, but not even Solomon in all his glory was laid out as President Wondershrub is now laid out like a beached salamander on this cold sepulcher before us . The lessons for us could not be clearer, if only we would but harken unto them.

Let this Groundhog Day, with its promise of springtime for the meek and humble of heart, serve to remind us of our Founders' origins, to remember forever this special day that restoreth to us, in this hallowed park, the promised Hundredfold of Eden, and re-planteth, in this blest soil, before our very eyes, the Tree of Knowledge of Good and Evil, and entrusteth us, in this sacred hour, here at this much visited Tower of Babel, with Adam's very own Apple for safekeeping. It is exactly as was foretold, that which has been lost has been foundeth, that which was begat sits now fully begotten before our very eyes.

All eyes closed, now. Voices stilled. Heads bowed low. Fingers touching our lowliest toes. Stomachs sucked completely in. Prostates in hand, let us reflect on the letter W and its wondrous messages begat by him who lies here under glass as meek as *fois gras*, so disfigured and yet so Raptured before our very eyes. Let us pray that we, too, be freed from our Babelonian captivity, liberated from our enemies' destructive jackhammers, and returned to our Founders' Promised Land, just as were the Chosen People freed in their own day from Pharaoh's jackhammers in their own Babylonian Captivity . *(reflects in silence).*

Open now thy eyes, unbow thy heads, release thy humblest toes, ungird thy stomachs and unhand thy prostates. Let us, as one united people, rise and gird our loins with loincloths black in mourning, to escort this Wonder from this holy chapel in the NASCAR funeral cortege to his final resting place amongst the gilded lilies of the field, by the flowing Waters of Shiloh, beside this ancient Tower of Babel, in this very Garden of Eden Theme Park he so longed to see, while begetting, in this day of such lamentation and inauguration, such Wonder upon us and upon all bewildered peoples everywhere. Amen.

15

Inaugural Address of President Lip Surley

President Surley's Inaugural Address occurs at the prow of the Visitor Center Ark in the center of the Garden of Eden Theme Park adjoining the South Lawn of the White House. The address is broadcast worldwide exclusively via the studios of FAUX TV permanently located in the residential quarters in the White House. The two bipartisan commentators are Really Unruly and guest commentator Stephen Cobalt, in communication with on-site reporters in the field.

President Surley arrives in an entourage of black stretch Hummer limos flying Hallibuttox flags. The President's Hummer is towing a red, white and blue lion's cage in which Osama bin Laden is sitting. President Surley wears a Phantom of the Opera cape and a Phantom mask on one side of his face. He strides, grimacing, to the podium erected on the prow of the Ark. There he is joined by Secretary Brunette Brunhilde, Inspector Alonzo Gonzo, Secretary Nostradamus, Secretary Windy, Field Marshall Rumpelstilskin Emeritus, Reverend Rasputin, the Sturgeon General and former Inspector General Johnny Ashpit, the Joint Chiefs Combo, the Supreme Court's Anvil Chorus and the Environmental Protection Agency Minstrel Singers. The People's Halleluiah Chorus is present but silent.

The Charwoman of the Joint Chefs of Staff serves the podium guests steroid-laced apple hors d'oeuvres arranged on a platter containing, under glass, the silverized head of former President Wondershrub. The GOP Symphony Orchestra, with Press Secretary Whiteout at the tuba, plays the dance theme from the "Oil Fever Polka."

Really Unruly, FAUX NEWS:

Here we are, Stephen, in our FAUX broadcast booth for this solemn inaugural address being broadcast exclusively by FAUX NEWS from the presidential bedroom on this special Groundhog Day. What a fair and balanced day for all patriots and evangelicals to assemble! There's nothing to be critical about today, Steve.

Stephen Cobalt: Right you are, Really. A solemn testimonial to the loss of the much lamented President Wondershrub, the excision and silverizing of his tongue and elongated nose, and the emplatterment of his head, and the ascent to that high office by former Vice President Surley. We will have much to remember about this lovely spring day.

Really: Steve, yes, exactly, what a thrill to be here on Groundhog Day as former Vice President Lip Surley is now about to ascend onto the Ark's deck to assume the mantle of his predecessor in office, the very literary President Wondershrub, whose passing casts the pall borne earlier today by his compassionate pallbearers.

Certainly one of the things our viewing audience will be watching closely today is whether Our Lord Surley can manage a smile or some form of genuine human contact. I think His Majesty will make an effort to rise to this challenge! And challenge it is! A challenge especially facing him today before this sellout crowd of entrepreneurs, economists, pipeline owners, market analysts, oil tycoons, and futures analysts, all invited here to witness their business partner assume the nation's highest office, and all this in the presence of the much-sought-after Osama bin Laden . What are the President's odds of pulling off anything like a smile for this audience, Steve?

Cobalt: Well , it would be hard to tell under that Phantom mask he's wearing, Really. But for another view of the smile issue, let's go down to our FAUX play- by- play announcer on the field, Dohnny Boy and our on-site Oilman, Ole. Dohnny, what's the mood like down there by the Ark?

Dohnny Boy, FAUX SPORTS: Really and Stephen, that's exactly it. President Surley and his lip have been in training for many years for today's Groundhog Day. He's worked out with the best of the handshaking politicians in the nation's capital, in the halls of Congress, on the fields of Mars, and especially with the nation's Secret Energy

Task Force, not to mention taking graduate ventriloquist weight training and repeated Dale Carneige courses on making and keeping friends. He's certainly done the heavy lifting for today's big event. With that background he's not likely to cower before competition, Really, especially for a big event such as this. I think our viewers can anticipate a smiling display of the highest caliber today. And, from what we can barely see under his mask, it looks like his lip has finally taken a turn for the better, with less of a sneer.

Word has it that his best friend, Field Marshall Rumpelstilskin Emeritus, this very morning, in preparation for him assuming this high office, honored him with the intimate personal service of injecting porcine and bovine steroids into both his ample buttocks. And rumor has it that the Field Marshall has nominated President Surley to be Chief Auctioneer at the next round of OPEC oil bidding What good friends! And what lovely presidential gifts!

Really Unruly: Thanks, Dohnny Boy, for those penetrating insights about His Majesty. Let's now go to dockside, near the prow of the Ark, to hear from our man by the boat, as it were, Moby.

Moby, FAUX Field Announcer: Really, Dohnny, and Steve, too, what a thrill to be here on the dock, right here adjoining this new Biblical Theme Park, by the South Lawn, by this massive Ark, with the statute of Noah right on the prow of this great ship, with this sell-out crowd of entrepreneurs, corporate tycoons and marketeers so pin-striped before us! Truly capital! I think I hear in the background the Messiah University Church Lady Choir beginning to hum "That Old Rugged Cross." Back to you, Really.

Really: Just moments ago His Eminence President Surley emerged from the Hell Hole tunnel in the Garden of Eden Theme Park. Then, after allowing all in the assembly to see his shadow, he was driven here, alone, in his stretch Hummer limo, in the company only of his chauffeur, with Osama bin Laden in tow behind him in a lion's circus cage. The other members of his administration immediately thereafter arrived in their own stretch Hummers . I understand these are the latest hybrid vehicles, Stephen, that get up to 3 mpg on highways.

Now, as I look toward the Ark's great deck, I see Our Lordship approaching the podium. He is preceded by five robed Supreme Court Justices bearing lighted candles. The President mounts the deck and now stands near the Ark's great wheel beside its control panels displaying the "on" and "off" buttons operating all water and pipeline services here. He is now joined by the combined choirs of the Federal Courts of Appeal and the chorale of the Department of State, as well as the tumblers of the Environmental Protection Agency and the famed Robert Patrickson Liturgical Dancers.

Now I think we're going to witness the coronation and "Presentation of the Gifts." President Surley is standing at the altar-like table before the Ark's wheel, his cape rippling majestically in the breeze, his Mona Lisa half-smile barely visible under his Phantom mask. His cabinet officials stand smartly a short distance behind him on the deck, Secretary Brunhilde nearest to him. Now, with a trumpet flourish, Justices Scorpio and Scorpolini of the Supreme Court, wearing their black robes, approach the President carrying a purple pillow bearing a golden crown. Justice Scorpio takes the crown and places it reverently on the gleaming dome of President Surley. He recites to the President the solemn words of presidential authority inscribed on the crown: "Thou art a Branch Unto Thyself."

Now the CEOs of the world's major oil, drug and water corporations begin to line up and ascend the steps, each escorted by a lithesome liturgical dancer in red-white-and-blue tutus along with a candle-bearing Supreme Court Justice. They process to the table before His Liege. They bow before him and place on the table complimentary gifts memorializing this great occasion -- Collector's Editions of Hallibuttox Premium and High Viscosity Oils, 20 vials of Hallibotox Skin Repair, and now, from the country's drug manufacturers, a Six Pack of Bovine Steroids, and from Waste Management Inc., an embossed container of lip balm drawn from his many liposuction procedures. What thoughtful gifts!

Next comes Reverend Rover Rasputin. He mounts the stairs and places on the altar table a container of his latest line of purgatives named "Reverend Rover's Right-Minded Hogwash Expectorant." Next in line comes the President of the NRA, the famous real life actor Ben Hur, who places on the gift table an engraved bulls-eye for use on the President's next hunting trip plus an ammunition belt with hundreds of secret compartments. Now former Inspector General Johnny Ashpit, also liturgically escorted, ascends to the podium carrying his offerings to the new president. Moby, can you see what they are?

Moby, on the Field Play-by-Play Announcer: Yes, Steve and Really, I certainly can. The former Inspector General, as you know, while in that office in the Justice Department, became something of an entrepreneur. While serving as Inspector General, he started his own line of "Just-Us Lingerie" for covering up the exposed breasts of naked statues and portrait figures. It looks like he's offering the new President a large-busted brassiere from his firm's intimate product line, embossed on one side with the scales of justice, on the other with a semi-automatic hunting rifle.

Now Inspector Ashpit walks over to the microphone and joins Ms Annabelle Nastycolt as they take up their song sheets. Let's listen in as they sing an alternating duet from the official Marine anthem, "From the Halls of Montezuma, To the Shores of Tripoli." (*they sing, alternating verses*)

Really Unruly: How beautiful! I think Reverend Heartfelt is now about to give the invocation for His Majesty. Let's listen.

Reverend Heartfelt: Heavenly Father of us all, we just come before you this lovely spring day, named after the Goundhog whose feast we also honor today, to ask you to be with your newly anointed President, now become your Chosen One It was of this very Chosen One that the prophet Isaiah wrote:

> I will ascend to heaven, I will raise my throne above the Stars of God. I will sit enthroned on the mount of assembly, on the utmost heights of the sacred mountain. I will ascend above the tops of the clouds. I will make myself like unto the Most High. (Is., 14: 12-14)

We now just ask you, O Loving Father, to guide and guard him, to give him wisdom and age and grace, and a genuine smile. Direct him, we pray, away from all burning bushes and surging waters and help his lips display a presidential smile, even under his mask, all the days of his life. In Your Name, Amen.

Stephen Cobalt: Former Inspector General Ashpit now ascends the podium again escorted by a lovely liturgical dancer. He appears to be wearing a bishop's miter. He curtseys before the President. Now he takes his sacred oils, lifts the presidential crown, and anoints the President's smooth bald head with 30-weight Special Edition Inaugural Oil.

Now the CEOs of Hallibuttox, OPEC and Enron approach the podium and, with the help of Field Marshall Emeritus Rumpelstilskin and the Rasputin Liturgical Dancers, they place laurel wreaths of garlands around his neck. Each garland is strung with miniature oil cans autographed personally by the CEOs of Exxon, Gulf, Shell, Sinclair and Standard Oil and strung with pink orchids specially grown in our Iraqi garland gardens.

Now, as the President adjusts these garlands around his cape, I see Former Inspector General Johnny Ashpit coming forward again. His firm, we understand, has recently expanded its lingerie services worldwide to include other intimate apparel to cover park statutes, museum paintings, and other naked works of art, in accord with the Biblical injunction to "clothe the naked." Inspector Ashpit mounts the stairs leading to the podium, genuflects, and approaches the President. He offers the President an official Presidential Loincloth in speedo style, embroidered in gold with the presidential seal and, we understand, containing multiple secret compartments for holding presidential secrets! Inspector Ashpit bows before him, descends the podium stairs and returns to his front-row seat on the dias.

Now the richly-gifted President approaches the microphones with his response to the lovely invocation of a moment ago. Let's listen in.

President Surley: I respond to you now with the prayer of Jabez: "Oh, that you would bless me in deed and enlarge my territory, that Your hand would be with me and keep me from those who threaten my ownership."

Dohnny Boy: What a truly pious invocation! And such a capital responsorial, from Jabez no less! Escorted by his candle-bearing colleagues, Justice Antediluvian Scorpio now comes forward to administer the oath of office to his hunting partner who has been such a loyal tutor to him in so many of his difficult Supreme Court decisions. He too curtseys before the president. Let's listen in.

Justice Scorpio: "You do solemnly swear to tell your citizens the truth, the whole truth, and nothing but the truth, as long as it is entrepreneurial and cosmetic. You promise to love, honor and obey the Constitution of your choice, to wiretap and waterboard only those who are in sickness and health, in good times and in bad, from this day forward, in your administration's hospitable gulags, all the days of your monarchy, until the sun sets on your oil fields and alternative energy sources do ye part." If you agree, say "I do."

President Surley: Amen.

Really: Little Sir Echo of our FAUX studios now approaches His Highness and places a royal scepter of gold directly in his right hand, as a symbol of absolute submission to his wishes. Sir Echo prostrates himself before President Surley and pledges his oath of absolute fidelity. He now returns to his seat on the dias. I think we are now about to hear from President Surley himself. Let's listen.

President Surley:

Fellow consumers, we are met here today on the prow of this great oil-powered Ark, in the spirit of its builder, Noah, to overcome any sympathy for former President Wondershrub so efficiently raptured from us by market forces beyond his control. His body lies before us among the lilies at the Tower of Babel but he no longer serves as a role model to any of us. He depleted his own health savings plan, a plan equally available both to the very rich like me, and equally to the poor, like him. He deserves no special collection for his health care costs, apart from the taxpayer funds used to emplatter his silverized head and elongated nose, both lying so eloquently on this platter .We must not wallow in sorrow for his passing from this White House to his whitened sepulcher. I let him pretend to be the Decider but in fact he played the Dupe. His departure is a cause of joy for the many wondrous lessons he leaves us What are those lessons? The first is to don our workplace uniforms and march toward the market goals his administration sought to achieve but failed : an ownership society without any government control, indeed, without any government at all beyond unfettered market forces surveyed from above by your nation's monarch.

All that has happened to President Wondershrub happened for reasons beyond your understanding. Only unnamed high government economists in the executive branch of government know these reasons, which remain confidential in my several secret compartments, where

I keep the nation's libido as well as my own. You, the American People, need not know these government events that touch you so directly, for your own good, I must add. That's the true meaning of democracy. Don't go to hell without it.

I can tell you one of the few things you are entitled to know about your monarchy. As to the rumor that it was I who arranged for the killing of President Wondershrub with a band of insurgents disguised as Belgian tourists, such speculation deserves no response for it is totally out of line. It is pure "hogwash" to surmise someone so compassionate as I could be capable of torturing and waterboarding him simply for saying that "our addiction to oil must stop."

As I proclaimed when the Wondershrub administration won its first popular election in the Supreme Court, this administration can do whatever we want. Machiavelli would have it no other way. For those neurotic civil rights lawyers who never stop questioning our authority, let it be repeated, as I said at President Wondershrub's coronation, my administration has all the legal authority we need to do whatever we want. In fact, we don't need any authority beyond this crown, gown and mask I wear today. My office exists apart and, indeed, above all branches of the Tree of Knowledge of Good and Evil, indeed, above all branches of government itself.

While some elite academics see this country as a democracy dedicated to free speech, my administration knows that free speech consists of a right of free thoughts, not of free speaking. A true market democracy thrives unfettered by government control except for those controls restraining free speech and leaking of secrets, each of which is sufficiently unpatriotic to merit a death sentence. This rule especially applies to any restrictions on market-driven energy consumption. Years ago, when Vice President Nelson Rockefeller, supported by President Ford, pushed a plan to have the government develop alternative sources of energy to reduce our dependence on oil, I scotched it. That remains one of my proudest achievements, as important to me as was former President Dioxin's sacred tongue to President Wondershrub.

As to the rumor that I served as ventriloquist for President Wondershrub to announce his administration's continuing wars and victories, these too are rumors leaked without permission of this administration. Each deserves but one answer: "Hogwash!" My expertise as a trained ventriloquist holding the Darth Vader Chair at the National Ventriloquism Institute was also leaked illegally to the press You will curse the day you fail to perform the punishing of leakings I have demanded! As to this latest leaking, those responsible for this leaking will burn in this park's Hell Hole to the full extent of the law. We are, as you may sometimes forget, a nation of laws, not of men, until we decide the latter is more important. I will decide that, for I am now your monarch and no one else is. We will remain first in war, first in peace, and first in covert operations. This is our due.

Some in the elite northeastern press have questioned my facial features. What they call my perpetual sneer actually results from my having to share a small part of my wealth with those who are less wealthy. I could easily arrange for my lip deformity to be surgically excised and replaced with a smile but that would require making my health records public, which the public shall never see. Wiretapping citizens may be a necessity but not any such invasion of my privacy.

On the subject of war, make no mistake about it. We won the election so we can do what we want. We in this administration wanted our wars in Iraq and Belgium so that I too, like Wondershrub, could serve my country on the front lines, as I always hoped to do, despite other priorities requiring my five deferments. Thanks to our services to this war effort, I am proud to say that all our worldwide enemies wallow in their last throes. We have no need of working with other nations. My administration will get rid of everything multi – multi- lateral treaties, multi-lateral institutions, multi-lateral alliances. Multi means wobby and caviling and sharing authority, things monarchs don't do. Why be multi- when we can be uni-?

President Wonderscrub's passing gives us no cause for sorrow. For one thing, he shattered the myth of white male supremacy. For another, he was unfaithful to the values of our English Founders who knew the true meaning of an all-powerful monarch. For another, he failed to privatize our social security system in accord with my guidelines for health savings plans. My administration will see to it that social security becomes much more efficient after we inaugurate my market-based program of euthanizing the elderly.

Let me tell you some of the goals of this administration. Contrary to the clatter of the elite liberal press, we are indeed dedicated to the environment. The global warming problem is not heat but anti-competitive humility. To that end, we plan to proudly extend the annual NASCAR races beyond Glacier Memorial National Park to entirely new asphalt raceways extending from the lodge at Yellowstone National Park, through the Grand Tetons, and into Glacier and back. Indeed, within the term of this administration every one of our National Parks will have asphalt NASCAR race tracks and NRA shooting ranges! Members of the NRA will patrol every one of our national parks and forests with their assault weapons to take out animals needed for food and oil. Many of these NRA sharpshooters I myself have had the honor to train and hunt with, and most have survived. Does a President shoot in the woods or not?

My administration will replace the entire Department of Justice with a new cabinet position known as the Department of Blind Trust. The lawyers' sole job in that office will be to find ways for me to do what I want. These lawyers will model their jobs on that of Inspector General Alonzo Gonzo, who will resume his rightful role as the Court Jester. The former Secret Service will assume a new name as "Secrets Service," whose covert operatives will deposit all government information in secret vials to be opened 200 years from now, to then be made available to the public, for my heirs' profit, as my own line of "Surley's Secrets." Not even the Good Lord Himself can see into these secret vials now. Do not be alarmed, my friends; my precedent for keeping and selling presidential secrets resides in Victoria's own successful marketing of her secrets. If Victoria can market her secrets for profit, no less should be true of the secrets of your monarch.

Religious and moral values remain at the top of our hierarchy. To that end my administration will expand this Garden of Eden Theme Park to every one of our national parks, and, indeed, to our newly expanded North and South Pole beaches, and also to the grounds around all of our embassies worldwide, with free admissions for clergy as well as for military personnel maimed in our wars spreading democracy to all nations of the world . Solomon himself reminds us that "When there is no vision, the people perish."

Make no mistake about it, what some see as the tragedy of 9/11 in reality constitutes a great blessing . If 9/11 didn't exist, my administration would have had to create it. Terrorism has given us a reason for implementing the very measures my administration planned before 9/11 to control the thoughts of elite free thinkers, like those Yale professors who flunked me out. We needed 9/11 to pass the Patriot Act, heighten surveillance, increase terrorism alerts, augment public fear, heighten militarism, inaugurate wiretapping and eavesdropping and expand waterboarding, my personal favorite. All these changes would have been impossible without the fears generated from 9/11. If 9/11 had not occurred, this administration would have had to create it by executive privilege, which I alone have the privilege to define, though I am not part of the executive branch.

We need to thank Osama bin Laden for helping do our work for us. President Wondershrub's repeated searches for Osama have now succeeded. Osama, in fact, has been contacted by our intelligence agents and brought here today at my request. Given his prowess in finding secret hiding places, I am happy to announce to you that Osama will hold a cabinet position in my administration as Chief of Staff and Secretary of Covert Operations, with supervision over all intelligence services. Come here, Osama! (*Kisses and embraces him*). For any of you in the congregation thinking he may have committed any crimes, I announce to you today that I have pardoned him his crimes, whatever they may have been, and have commuted his excessive sentence in return for his service in my administration. This is the fullest meaning of justice: Judge not lest you be judged!

What has this country learned? Probably nothing has been learned by you, my fellow consumers, but much has been learned about government. The American People are cripples, unable to embrace Mayberry Machiavellis or even climb the lowest branches on the Tree of Knowledge of Good and Evil. That tree's original location in Iraq had to be replaced with a Hallibuttox pipeline. The oil derrick now pumping oil in the original Eden will expand our energy resources beyond any concerns about good and evil. The American people must learn that its president enjoys the royal privileges of James II: the right to torture, to wiretap, to suppress, to massacre, to subjugate just as our Founding Fathers inherited from the Mother Country, (without the wigs and hats, however),   provided that we do so in the names of patriotism, democracy, and executive privilege, under a campaign of spreading democracy where it is lacking, including to indecent democracies such as Belgium.

Let me tell you some more things you don't really deserve to know about this administration's Happy Days energy policy. I don't have to tell you who the National Security Agency is spying on or how they're doing it. I can tell you that they won't spy on someone like me or my Secrets Service officers. I don't have to tell anything about the conduct of the war on terrorism. You should be content to know that the White House will soon be totally privatized and its press office moved to a Trappist monastery, with my new press secretary a monk vowed to permanent silence. Anyone who leaks information about gulags and surveillance will be hunted down as lacking in patriotism. Roses are red, Violets are blue, Leak something I don't approve, I'll shoot you too! Besides, any true patriot would rather go hunting with me than riding with Senator Kennedy.

We must emphasize our common bonds with our friends. Our administration has much in common with Iraq and Iran and other fundamentalist countries and, indeed, with our pardoned friend Osama here today: Devotion to one God, Allah; subjection to an all-powerful monarch under a divine right government; disdain for pluralism; suppression of questioning and dissent; adherence to literal texts as authoritative truth; cosmetic legislative and judicial functions; use of torture to gain information; use of symbols of democracy to mask war; punishing those who criticize patriotism and virtue as unnamed high government officials dictate; and fusing religious and political authority into one executive branch of government under my control but of which I am not a part. Our goal in this country exactly matches the goals of George III, indeed, of my friend Osama: government works best when its monarch is above the law and its citizens think exactly as their government tells them, without leaks, without questioning, without knowledge but with blind patriotism.

Our ideals today transcend those of our Founders. Those once-revered Founders actually got a lot about this country wrong. Indeed, our true ideals more closely match those of Osama: we both are engaged in a Manichean struggle where Sons of Light confront Sons of Night, where citizens must choose one infallible side against total evil, without middle ground between Absolute Truth and Absolute

Error, without dissent or contradiction or free speaking. This freedom is not our Founders' creation but a gift from Allah himself. Our government, like those of Osama and George III, is doing God's work from the top down. The one Absolute is father of the other.

We have other priorities than catering to thinking Elites. To those who disagree with my goals , I can only repeat what I said so forthrightly to my enemies on the very floor of the United States Senate: *(Secretary Brunhilde rushes to his side, shaking her head violently; he pushes her aside).* As I was saying, for those of you who see it differently, as I said on the floor of our pitiable Senate: "Go Fuck Yourselves!"

Really Unruly: Wow, Steve, that's a word we don't hear often down on the playing field. I know His Majesty used that term to address folks in Congress but here on the world's stage at his own inaugural, well, that's another matter.

Stephen Cobalt: Exactly right, Really. We don't hear words like that on the playing fields, except on rare times from those who drop their bratwurst. Wow, look at that giant Vulture swooping down from the sky! He has something in his mouth! It's an Apple, and, as I look more closely, I think I see a withered A on it! This Demon Vulture has swooped down onto the Ark and now perches right on its prow! Look, this Vulture is now offering the Apple to President Surley! Secretary Brunhilde tries to push the great bird away but it snaps at her. The President and the Vulture are whispering something privately. Now look, President Surley has taken a bite! He passes the Apple to his cabinet members, and each follows his command to take a bite! And now, perhaps for the first time in his life, he's actually smiling, indeed, from ear to ear! No more Mona Lisa smile, to be sure. What a treat for our cameras!

Oh, oh, now it's becoming just the opposite -- chewing the Apple has dislodged the President's mask from where it covered his jaw. We can now see fully, for the first time today, the surgical implant dispensing high-grade Hallibotox liposuction directly into the President's deformed lip! The President is not happy to be unmasked. He's no longer smiling but beginning to grimace in pain, more than usual!. He's hurling the Apple away. He seems to feel shame, not something we've ever seen in him. I see little beads of skin oil breaking out on his brow, like Adam and Eve experienced as they were leaving Paradise.

Dohnny Boy, *on the Field*: Really and Steve, look at that throw! The President has thrown the Apple away in disgust, but it's somehow bounced off the Tree of Knowledge and ricocheted against the "On" button on the control panel operating the flood walls and compost pipelines around us.   The large glass pipelines containing melting glacier water are starting to open! Melted glacier waters are beginning to sweep across the theme park from the Potomic! The economists, marketeers and tycoons in the audience are rapidly scrambling for higher ground. The Ark is now straining at its moorings. It's starting to drift in the direction of the Falls just before the Jonah the Whale Exhibit!

Really Unruly: This could be trouble!. Moby, can you get closer and give us a first- hand account of what's taking place down there?

Moby, *on the bank near Jonah*: Pandemonium on the deck, Really. The surging glacier waters are sweeping in from the Potomic, entering the Theme Park and now crashing over the Falls. The Ark is floating free of its moorings. It now broadsides the Tree of Knowledge of Good and Evil! The Tree's lower branches   poke a gaping hole in its hull! The pairs of the seven   surviving animals – rhinos, hippos , whatever -- are escaping into the surging torrents!

Fighting is breaking out on the top deck for control of the Ark. Secretary Brunhilde pushes the Field Marshall into the surging waters! The Sturgeon General has just fallen overboard. The Field Marshall is shouting something like – let me get closer to get this right – "alle Menschen werden Bruder." No one seems to be listening. Inspector Gonzo, Secretary Windy and Osama bin Laden are struggling for control of the helm. President Surley now pushes them away, off the deck, and into the surging waters, right at the highest point of the Falls. Justice Scorpio, still wearing his judicial robes, is shouting "Miserere nobis," but no one is coming to his aid. Inspector Gonzo struggles in the water – he reaches for a floating law book bobbing in the waves but it won't support him! Reverend Rasputin is grasping for a floating bottle of his purgative oil -- it seems unable to hold him! The surging waves have stripped off his clothes right down to his bikini! Secretary Windy and the Sturgeon General are trying to mount the rhinos and hippos frolicking in the torrent, but now they're being bucked off ! And Osama's robes are making it impossible for him to swim! Former

Inspector Ashpit has found some holy oils -- it looks like he's now anointing the bald pate of the President, perhaps as some sort of last rite!

Now the President himself is running to grab the Ark's helm. Opps, he's slipped on an oil slick on the prow right by the coin-operated glacier fountain. He's lost his step and can't grab the ship's wheel ! He's fallen into the surging waves! He reaches to grab a branch of the Tree of Knowledge of Good and Evil, but it won't hold him! It won't support him at all!

Now the Ark is passing directly over the bodies of Inspectors Ashpit and Gonzo who, it turns out, have also lost their clothes. The waters are sweeping Secretary Heartfelt and Reverends Fallsoon and Patrickson into the Rapture Ready Ride -- they're now being catapulted high into the sky!

The Ark's now careening directly into the Y pipeline junction just below the Falls. Inspector Gonzo has been clinging onto the levers of the Justice Shredder but now he's being sucked into its blades with Osama, a homestyle execution indeed! Justice Scorpio, who just moments ago was singing so happily with President Surley, is now pinned against the gigantic gyrating silver tongue at the Tower of Babel -- the silver tongue is battering his head back and forth against the Tower! Secretary Heartfelt and the Sturgeon General are trying to grab ahold of the rhinos and hippos swimming in the flood, but these animals are pulling them under water! A raging whirlpool is sucking the Field Marshall Emeritus and Reverend Fallsoon directly into the Park's Hell Hole! Oh, the horror!

President Surley has now lost all his clothes – he's buck naked right down to his speedo loincloth with its multiple secret compartments! The weight of secrets in those compartments is pulling him under! Look at all that body hair on his back and those steroid injection tracks on his buttocks! He's bobbing about just before the great mouth of Jonah, beyond the reach of the anointing rituals of Inspector Ashpit and the Secrets Service officers who have plunged into the torrent to protect his loincloth secrets   And over there, on the opposite bank, the surging waters of the Falls are carrying Reverend Rover Rasputin directly against his floating table of discounted purgative lotions, and now he's being swept head-first directly into the "Adam " restroom!

The President is having a difficult time of it. I don't think he's as talented a swimmer as he was a shooter. Oh, now another surprise: the demonic Great Vulture itself has come back, is hovering over the struggling President as he's nearing Jonah's jaws! This Great Bird swoops down toward the President in his agony, alights on his shoulders, and, look at that, Steve and Really, this Vulture now is kissing, embracing and caressing the President, licking his wounds, cooing at him affectionately, as though to comfort or perhaps to welcome him .

Moby, On- the- Field announcer, *near the Jonah Exhibit*: But even this friendly Vulture can't save the President! He's now being swept directly against Jonah's great lips and waterboarded up and down repeatedly! Oh, now he's being swept right into Jonah's open gullet! Jonah is lighting up like a pinball machine, smiling, his neon eyes laughing, as his jowls begin to close and chew. I now hear Jonah humming "Pomp and Circumstance."

Stephen: Dohnny, can you get around to the back side of Jonah and tell us exactly what's happening back there?

Dohnny Boy: Yes, Stephen , I can. I'm now at the back end of the glass Jonah Exhibit where, thanks to the administration's open pipeline policy, we have an unobstructed view inside Jonah's belly . The roters are turning and there's great noise , banging and thrashing. The sludgehammers are churning away! Human oil is now beginning to course through the oil pipelines which act as Jonah's intestines. Globs of compost are exiting Jonah's backside! Huge, foul smelling compost! It's piling up like a Texas mountain and surging onto this conveyer belt right at the entrance to the Theme Park.

Really: Ole, you're our Hallibuttox oil expert and you're right on the scene at the back end of Jonah. Can you see what's happening there ?

Ole: Oh, Stephen and Really, I can. The President is now being sucked through the series of sludgehammers , jackhammers, and waterboarding devices inside Jonah's belly. I can see his bloated body being cut up and dissected and compressed as we speak! Water and oil are flowing, you might say, like Justice itself! The oil coming from the President's compressed remains – well, there's got to be several tankers in each buttock! It looks to be of a very low grade. But look at all the compost! All this rich compost from the ample body of the President is now oozing out the tail end of Jonah, with a rancid odor. It's flowing in the direction of the Jefferson Memorial, while the President's copious bodily oils are surging directly into the oil pipelines, enough probably for the entire third world of Texas. What an alternative energy source, Really! The President's body seems entirely composed of oil, though Jonah's computerized dials show it's actually an oil-steroid alloy.

Really Yes, Ole, I can see now the compost being carried out the tail end of Jonah on the National Park conveyer belt heading toward the nearby monuments. Can you get close enough to tell us which monument is receiving this enriched compost, Dohnny? What does it say?

Dohnny Boy: Let me get closer to read it if I can. Gad, the stench is overwhelming. Yes, I can make my way up to it and now I can see that monument. It's the Jefferson Memorial monument, all lit up for these inaugural ceremonies I'm getting close enough now to see this compost piling up around the lilies of the field at its base.

Really Unruly: Whose monument is it, and what does the monument say?

Ole: It's the Thomas Jefferson Memorial Monument, with one of his best known quotations inscribed in bold letters right on its face. I can read it to you:

> A little patience and we shall see the reign of witches pass over, their spells dissolve, and the people, recovering their true sight,restore their government to its true principles. It is true that in the meantime we are suffering deeply in spirit and incurring the horrors of a war and long oppressions of enormous public debt. If the game runs sometimes against us at home we must have patience til luck turns, and then we shall have an opportunity of winning back the principles we have lost, for this is a game where principles are at stake.
>
> Thomas Jefferson

Stephen Cobalt: And now, for the first time, Really, I'm hearing the People's Hallelujah Chorus break into song. Why, listen, they're singing the "Great Amen" from Handel's *Messiah*. Let's all join in!

Printed in the United States
118017LV00002B/184/A